NAMELESS GIRL

A DETECTIVE CHARLOTTE PIERCE NOVEL

KATE GABLE

BYRD BOOKS

COPYRIGHT

Visit my website at www.kategable.com

**BE THE FIRST TO KNOW ABOUT MY
UPCOMING SALES, NEW RELEASES
AND EXCLUSIVE GIVEAWAYS!**

W ant a Free book? Sign up for my
Newsletter!

Sign up for my newsletter:

https://www.subscribepage.com/kategableviplist

Join my Facebook Group:
https://www.facebook.com/
groups/833851020557518

Bonus Points: Follow me on BookBub and
Goodreads!

https://www.goodreads.com/author/show/
21534224.Kate_Gable

ABOUT KATE GABLE

Kate Gable loves a good mystery that is full of suspense. She grew up devouring psychological thrillers and crime novels as well as movies, tv shows and true crime.

Her favorite stories are the ones that are centered on families with lots of secrets and lies as well as many twists and turns. Her novels have elements of psychological suspense, thriller, mystery and romance.

Kate Gable lives near Palm Springs, CA with her husband, son, a dog and a cat. She has spent more than twenty years in Southern California and finds inspiration from its cities, canyons, deserts, and small mountain towns.

She graduated from University of Southern California with a Bachelor's degree in Mathematics. After pursuing graduate studies in mathematics, she switched gears and got her MA in Creative Writing and English from Western New Mexico University and her PhD in Education from Old Dominion University.

Writing has always been her passion and obsession. Kate is also a USA Today Bestselling author of romantic suspense under another pen name.

Write her here:

Kate@kategable.com

Check out her books here:

www.kategable.com

Sign up for my newsletter:
https://www.subscribepage.com/kategableviplist

Join my Facebook Group:
https://www.facebook.com/
groups/833851020557518

Bonus Points: Follow me on BookBub and Goodreads!

https://www.bookbub.com/authors/kate-gable

https://www.goodreads.com/author/show/
21534224.Kate_Gable

ABOUT NAMELESS GIRL

⭐⭐⭐⭐⭐ *"Gripping! Fascinating mystery thriller filled with intriguing characters and lots of twists and turns!"* *(Goodreads)*

When a 13-year-old girl vanished, her friends have kept certain details of that night a secret. Even though she was only a teenager, this mistake continues to haunt Detective Charlotte Pierce.

Twenty years later, Charlotte attends her middle school reunion and begins to investigate what happened to her friend that night.

Meanwhile, back home in Mesquite County, CA, another **teenager reports her sister missing and comes home to discover that both of her parents have been brutally murdered**.

Will Charlotte be able to locate the missing girl and find out who killed her parents and why?

Will Charlotte ever find out that truth about what happened to her friend that night?

This suspenseful thriller is perfect for fans of James Patterson, Leslie Wolfe, Lisa Regan, L. T. Vargus and Karin Slaughter. It has mystery, angst, a bit of romance and family drama.

Praise for Kate Gable's Girl Missing Series

⭐⭐⭐⭐⭐"Gripping! This book was a great read. I found a new author that I enjoy and I can't wait to read the rest of the series! " *(Goodreads)*

⭐⭐⭐⭐⭐ "The twists come at you at breakneck pace. Very suspenseful." *(Goodreads)*

⭐⭐⭐⭐⭐ "I really enjoyed the ins and outs of the storyline, it kept me reading so that I could find out how the story would turn out. And the ending was a major shocker, I never saw it coming. I truly recommend this book to everyone who loves mysteries and detective stories." *(Goodreads)*

⭐⭐⭐⭐⭐" I loved it. One of the best books I've ever read." - Amazon review

⭐⭐⭐⭐⭐ "I couldn't put the book down I give it a thumbs up and I would recommend it to other readers" *(Goodreads)*

★★★★★ "Another great book in the Kaitlyn Carr series! I am so drawn into these books. I love that they are not just about Kaitlyn's search for her sister but also about a case she is working on. I can't wait for the final book in the series!" *(Goodreads)*

1

FRANNY

My sister lived to dance. She didn't start out young. She took her first dancing class at ten and she fell in love. She told me once, when she still talked to me, that there was something about the music and the movement. It was the closest thing to flying with your feet planted on the ground.

I pick a lemon off the tree in our backyard and inhale its sour-sweet scent. It is covered by a thin layer of California desert dust and it makes my mouth water.

I look at the picture of my sister on my phone, the last one that I have. Her dance troupe, Company 11, a nondescript name for a place that she called home, was performing at a parade in Disneyland. My parents fought a lot when we were younger.

Different business ventures didn't go as planned, a house in foreclosure, and the one happy place for our whole family was Disneyland.

It's a two-hour drive, less than that really, and you're there spinning on rides, eating churros in a world consumed by magic, one that is far away from all of your problems. For others, Disneyland is a once-in-a-lifetime destination, but for Southern California residents like us, it's a local getaway.

On the occasion of this photo, Madison was dancing in the parade down Main Street. She's dressed in a yellow, chiffon dress that made her look like Tinker Bell. Her feet moved in cohesive steps with all of the others. Her hair was pulled back into a tight bun.

Everything about the ten girls was identical, and yet she stood out the way she always does.

Her big wide eyes.

The sprinkle of freckles across the bridge of her nose.

That day, Madison danced as if it were her last time, as if no one were watching. She couldn't have known it at the time, no one did, what was going to happen. She had always had bad stage fright but forced herself to dance anyway.

"It goes away after a few steps on the stage," she used to tell me. "That's when it's the worst, but once the music takes over and your body knows what to do, you let yourself float away."

Madison loved nothing more than to dance. It wasn't about glory or accolades or looking beautiful. Even though she enjoyed all of those things, it was about something else altogether.

Besides dance, Madison loved animals. When our parents got the house on two acres up in the hills, she was in heaven. Dad wasn't a big fan at first, but the goats and the little pig quickly won him over. Just like all of us, he was an animal lover at heart. My parents are not rich people and they scraped and saved to get this place.

We could have gotten a much better house down in the valley, more comfortable for less money. But they got this foreclosure, somewhat dilapidated, in need of a lot of work, because of the land and so that they could have animals. It is a hobby farm more than anything else. They like to say that this is a good place to retire eventually because "it'll keep you busy for years to come."

Mom and Dad have an accounting business in Palm Valley, a forty minute drive from doorstep-to-doorstep. The commute never bothered them much. Recently they've been working a lot from home, and

Madison seemed happy, too. After all the tumultuous times we endured for years, the money problems and everything else, I thought this year was actually going quite well.

The trip to Disneyland was the pinnacle of everything that made sense. We were happy. The four of us even rode the *Pirates of the Caribbean* together, enjoying the solitude and the serenity away from the madness that is sometimes that place.

And then, just three days later, Madison took off.

Left.

This wasn't the first time, and Mom and Dad were annoyed. She had friends all around and she often slept over at their houses, but this time it was different.

When Madison didn't come back on Monday, I told my parents that something was wrong. I could tell that they were worried as well, but were pretending that it was fine.

And then just like that, she was gone.

2

MADISON

I got there earlier than usual. My friends weren't back yet and I had the place to myself. I like being home. My sister's finally not getting on my nerves as much as she used to when she was little, but it's suffocating in a way. I can't wait to get a new place and to move out. The only problem is money.

When I can get a few nights stay at a friend's house it's always a nice relief. Stay up late, have a few drinks, smoke some weed, go out, meet some guys. What no one ever tells you about going to a local community college is that all of your friends will end up going to four-year universities like UCLA, USC, San Diego, or Ivy League schools out on the East coast and you're going to stay behind feeling like you already messed up your life. And you're not even nineteen years old.

My parents' argument for college was always about the importance of education and a four-year degree in order to do something meaningful with my life. It was a no-brainer that I would go away to school until it wasn't.

I mean, I make good money as a waitress at Desert Willow Country Club. Made a lot more than all my friends who went to universities, but I don't fit in. Most of the people in my college classes were adults, many with husbands and kids of their own. That is something that is far away in my future.

Meredith, Tyler, and Colby are the kids that I didn't exactly hang out with in high school. I was a straight A honor student who took lots of AP classes. They were, well, there's no other way to put it but *druggies*. They smoked weed early in the morning, skipped lots of classes, and had no plans for the future.

I met Colby at Desert Willow. She's pretty and tall, and is good at making older men feel at ease.

We started spending time together and I found out that Meredith's mom had kicked her out and now she is crashing with Colby and Tyler, who have been dating since the ninth grade and are now expecting a baby. Despite everything, and from how it looks on the outside, I think they'll be good parents. They've been together for a while and they really love each other.

Tyler isn't one to cheat. He likes video games too much. That's really all they do now that Colby can't drink or smoke weed, and we're all supporting her by not bringing it into the house.

My phone rings and it's Mom again. I talked to her yesterday and I know that I have to answer today for her to feel okay with everything.

"Yeah, I'm still here," I say. "Just hanging out with my friends."

"When are you planning on coming home?" she asks, annoyed.

"I have a lot of shifts back to back and then I just want to unwind and hang out with Colby and Meredith," I say, keeping the part about Tyler living here a secret.

After the uncomfortable conversation with way too many things left unsaid, I hang up and take a deep breath. Things with Mom have been tense on and off, depending on how involved she wants to be in my life. When she and Dad were working all of that overtime to try to save up for the house, they were never around. That was a good five years. Now, suddenly, they want to be involved. Suddenly, it's like I matter again.

No thanks, I want to tell her, but I stay quiet to keep the peace. She doesn't know about Tyler living here and she doesn't know about Colby being pregnant.

What she doesn't know isn't going to kill her. They're my friends. I'm nineteen. If I were at UCLA right now, or USC or San Diego State, she wouldn't be like this, in my business. She wouldn't be checking up on me every single day and night. But the truth is that I messed up. I didn't go, even though I had the acceptance letters and my parents willingness to co-sign a loan.

As I sit on this patched up Goodwill couch in a dusty old part of Palm Springs, I know that this place is a big step up for Colby and Tyler. They both grew up in crappy apartments and trailer parks, and it means everything to them to have a place of their own.

But it's a huge step down for me.

What am I doing here? It's been a year of this, and I should be done with my first year of college right now. Instead, what do I have to show for anything?

A lot of hours at the Country Club, a little bit of cash in my pocket that all went to pay for the new car and insurance that my parents refused to provide since they were paying for the roof over my head.

No, I deserve more than this. I pull out my phone and check the application deadlines. I only took two classes last semester and I'm in the middle of one this spring, but I'm not doing too well.

I look up the application deadlines to transfer. I know I'm not going to blow anyone away with my performance this year, but I have the essay and of the whole summer to make it up.

Maybe I can get back in. Maybe I don't have to tell them that I took classes this year and instead just say that I took a year off to work.

I imagine myself on the cliffs, feet buried in the sand, looking at the ocean. Santa Barbara and San Diego both sound amazing right about now. When I pull up the acceptance letters on my phone, I feel a huge pang of regret for what I did not do.

It's not a good feeling to be a failure at nineteen.

But people start over all the time in their thirties, forties, fifties, and even older. There's nothing wrong with that. Besides, we each have our own path to follow, right? I think, trying to convince myself of what is still possible.

Nevertheless, it all feels like my life is slipping away and nothing is ever going to change.

3

CHARLOTTE

The morning starts out rather atypically. I spill my coffee all over myself and have to change my outfit for work. I'm already running late and that just makes things a lot worse.

I overslept. I didn't end up doing yoga this morning like I had planned, breaking my five day streak of consistent workouts. Don't get too excited. I don't work out that often and so the habit tracker is an important thing in getting me to keep at it.

I had laid out the clothes that I was supposed to wear this morning last night because I was going to be meeting with the captain. It seemed like a casual invite for a morning chat until I mentioned it to my lieutenant, who said that it's anything but that. If I make a good impression, then I'll be given more consideration for a promotion, given that I pass the oral and written exams that is. And of course today, of all days, is the one when everything goes wrong.

Luckily I get to the station just in time, but I'm nevertheless frazzled. Imagine my relief when I show up, with my hair out of place, my thoughts frazzled and all over the place, and the secretary tells me that something came up and the meeting has been postponed.

"So how did it go?" Will asks when I get back to my desk and plop down on the squeaky chair.

"Luckily it didn't." I let out a deep sigh and longingly look over at the coffee maker which I have no energy to operate.

Will Torch is also a detective, a few years older than I am. We've been working together for over two years. We're a good complement to one another and this has been the most appropriate and professional relationship that I've ever been in. Given my track record, that's saying a lot.

"So you're saying that you're free for the foreseeable future?"

I sit up in the chair a little bit, looking at him. "You don't understand how stressful this was. The captain, just *me* and *him*, talking about my future prospects here."

"Oh, I have a very good idea of exactly what you're talking about, but now that it's canceled or postponed or whatever, you're about ready to do your job." Will smiles.

"I had plans to catch up on all this paperwork this morning," I say.

"What if you don't and do me a favor instead?" he asks, leaning over his desk and raising an eyebrow.

"I think I've done you plenty of favors, Will. Recently, seems like all I'm doing is favors for you."

"Yeah. Yeah. I know," he says, waving his hand.

He knows exactly what I'm referring to; his ongoing relationship with an old girlfriend who was only recently the primary suspect in the double murder of her ex-husband and new wife.

"Why don't you tell me what you have and I'll see if it's a favor I'm willing to do? In all seriousness, I do have a pile of paperwork to get through and the DA wants to prep me for court tomorrow."

"There's a girl here," Will points to the hallway. "sixteen years old, says her sister's missing. She wants to file a report."

"Isn't there anyone else that can do that?" I ask. "We have a whole department full of cops here."

"I think she needs to talk to a detective. She's certain that something bad has happened and I figured you'd be a good match. I have court this morning anyway," he says. "You know that."

"Okay, fine. If you really want..." I lean over in my chair to take a look at her. Her long dark hair is split in two braids like she's someone out of *Little House on the Prairie*.

"She looks twelve," I say.

"I know. That's why I didn't want to send her over to Nielson and Ramon. She needs a soft touch. She's never been in a police station before. Just talk to her."

"How old is her sister?" I ask. "Why aren't her parents making this report?"

"Her sister's older, nineteen. From what I heard, her parents aren't taking this as seriously as she is."

I shake my head. "She's probably at a friend's house."

"I know, but why don't you talk to the girl? Put her mind at ease and I think she can go home and we can forget all about this."

I take a swig of the leftover coffee from last night, which makes my face scrunch up. Somehow, I had forgotten how terrible stale coffee can be. I take a moment to pour myself a cup of fresh brew from the pot in the break room.

I watch her a little bit from the doorway. Her head is not buried in her phone. Instead, she just sits there with her hands wrapped around her knees, staring into space.

She's wearing a short sleeve paisley dress with jeans underneath. Honestly, it's hard to tell whether the dress is homemade or is the new style from Target where you look like you walked out of a 19th century farmhouse.

Walking over to her, I extend my hand. "Hi, I'm Detective Charlotte Pierce. I was told that your sister is missing."

"She's gone," she whispers.

"Why don't you come over here to my desk and we can sit down and you can tell me everything that's been going on?" I cut her off in mid-sentence.

"Madison just didn't come back one day. I don't even know where she could be. I called all of her friends. They all said that she was there, but then she took off and my parents don't think it's a big deal."

"Okay. Take a few deep breaths. First things first, please tell me your name."

"Franny Dillard," she says, looking up at me with her two huge, blue eyes.

4

CHARLOTTE

Franny Dillard is the type of girl who is not short on having things to say. As soon as we get to my desk and I grab her a chair and put her at the end, she opens her mouth, starts talking, and doesn't stop.

"Thank you again for letting me talk to you and for listening," Franny says, twisting her thumbs nervously. "I just had to come and tell you about what happened with my sister. I'm really worried."

"Okay," I say, glancing at the notes on my pad. "Let's go through it again."

"She was with her friends, Colby and Meredith. She goes over to their house often to sleep over and get away from things. Mostly on weekends. Mom and Dad are not happy with her this past year. Actually, last couple years, I guess. And it's been kind of hard."

"Can you tell me what's going on? Can you tell me the last time that you saw her?"

"It was April first, on Friday. That morning she told me she was going over there for the weekend. Mom was annoyed, but she promised to stay in touch. And Mom did talk to her that Saturday and Sunday on the phone, and she was there."

"Okay. So, what happened after that?"

"It's been three weeks, and I haven't heard a thing."

"Three weeks?" I ask.

"Yeah. Mom called Colby and she said that Madison had left that Sunday. We thought that she was staying there later through the week but apparently she took time off from Desert Willow. No one knows where she is now."

"Did your parents have a fight with Madison?"

"Yes." Franny nods her head. "They did."

"Did they kick her out?"

"They didn't kick her out, but they weren't happy that she was not sleeping at home. I mean, she's nineteen, but they expected her to check in. And she said that if she were going to college, they wouldn't expect that from her."

"Tell me more about that," I say.

"She's taking classes at the community college, but she is really smart. She got all straight A's. She aced her SAT's. And then senior year, she just said she didn't want to go away anymore. It was ridiculous. She got into UCLA, and UC Santa Barbara, University of Southern California."

"Maybe she wanted to get out of California?" I ask.

"If she did, why did she go to Desert Community College and just take two classes? And she wasn't doing very well in them, either. She was lying to my parents about her grades."

"What about you, Franny?" I ask. "How are you doing?"

"I get straight A's, and I want to go to Princeton," she says.

"All the way to New Jersey?"

She nods. "Yeah. I want to study chemistry and work in biotech. I've always been good at that kind of stuff."

"Well, I'm really proud of you. That's a really admirable goal," I say. "Can you tell me anything else? What about her phone? Social media?"

"She hasn't posted since that weekend, which is also ridiculous because she's addicted to Instagram and TikTok. She won't answer her phone."

"So, what do your parents think happened?"

"They think that she met some guy and took off. But just because Mom did that doesn't mean that Madison would've done it. She's not Mom."

"What do you mean?" I ask.

"Well, when my mom had just graduated from high school, she met this guy who was seven years older at the beginning of the summer. He was on his Harley and had plans to go to different music festivals all around the country that summer. He invited her to come and she said yes. Her parents were beyond themselves. She was from a small town in upstate New York, and you just didn't do that kind of thing. She was expected to go to college, get her degree, marry someone from the local community, and get into farming. But Mom didn't want that. This was the early 2000s. It was a different time, you know?"

I nod, smiling to myself about how not too far in the distance that seemed. And yet, the way that she spoke of it made it sound like it was the '70s or something.

"So what happened?"

"They spent the summer driving around the country and then moved in together in LA. She went to college and he supported her and later went as well. They got married, had us.

"Anyway, that guy my grandparents didn't want Mom to take up with is my dad. He was driving cross-country to start a new life in California. Opened a motorcycle shop, which didn't work out. But they ended up here after moving around LA and northern California for a bit. They're now accountants. They both got their degrees and opened a tax preparation business, which is doing quite well. And that's what helped them buy the land and the farm."

"The farm?"

"Yeah. Mom loves animals a lot and ended up exactly where her parents wanted her to be. But it's a hobby farm. We just have them as pets," Franny says. "We have three goats and a pig."

"So, your mom thinks that Madison did the same thing that she did?"

"Yeah, she does. I mean, she won't admit it, but she pretty much says that in so many words. But Madison isn't like her. She wouldn't make me worry. She would at least text me, or say where she's at. Mom and Dad didn't want me to come here and didn't want to make a report, but I just couldn't not do it. It's been long enough ... three weeks. I should have come that Monday that it happened, but I just kept waiting for her to come back. Is there anything you can do? Please."

She looks at me with her big, wide eyes.

———

I TAKE careful notes and double-check the spelling, the pictures, and the names. I promise to be in touch but she says that she wants to hang around and wait.

"When are you going to do the missing poster?" she asks. "Can I help you with that? I really want to make sure that everything is right."

"Well, before we can officially declare that she's missing, we really need a little bit more information," I say.

"What kind of information?"

"I need your parents to come in and give me a statement."

"Why? Is it because I'm under eighteen?"

"Yes, partly. And it's partly because she's an adult and she lives with them. Your mother could be right. She could be perfectly fine."

"I know that." Franny massages her knuckles. I look at her again. She's hunched over, letting the chair prop herself up. Her hair is a little wild even though it's in two loose braids. Her skin is clear but there isn't a smidge of makeup. She looks like she could easily pass for eleven or twelve, but definitely not sixteen.

From the pictures that she has shown me, Madison is the complete opposite.

Dark makeup, dark hair cut bluntly along the ears to make her look even older. There's one with a cigarette where she's dressed in androgynous clothing. Not just a pants suit, but an oversized one, reminding me a lot of Patti Smith. To say that she looks like she belongs more in 1970s New York City than in the middle of the desert in Mesquite County in 2022 is an understatement.

I look at the picture once more, trying to decide which one to put on the missing person poster. You want the picture to be representative of what the person looks like now. But if there's too much makeup and too much dressing up, that's not the best one to go with because that ends up being all that people see. So if she were to change her look, there's no way that she would be recognized.

"Do you have one where she is a little bit more natural?" I ask. "I think we might have to go with two pictures for the poster."

"So you are going to make one?"

"I'd encourage you to make one as well, but I will need to speak to your parents prior to this. Maybe they can give me some more information. You said your mom talked to her on the phone?"

"Yeah."

"And what did they talk about?"

"I'm not sure."

I don't want to Franny this, but I wonder how much her mother knows about what her eldest daughter's up to. She might be protecting her youngest from Madison's decisions.

"Look, I know what you're thinking," Franny says. "You look at me and think I'm a kid."

"No, I'm not saying that."

"Just because I don't dress up or wear makeup or heels or whatever, trying to pretend that I'm older than I am, doesn't mean that I'm all that innocent. I just want you to know that. I'm sixteen years old and I know what's going on. And I know that my sister probably had a boyfriend or a guy that my parents didn't want me to know about. But Colby and Meredith are not talking. You need to go talk to them. Maybe they'll say something to you."

"What's their address?" I ask.

She looks it up on her phone and shows me the screen and I jot it down. I know exactly where this is. It's in the dusty old part of Palm Valley. The one that was first developed around the 1950s. The houses here are full of character, but many have not aged. There's been an effort to revitalize them recently.

A lot of people are moving in from Los Angeles and San Francisco buying them up for what they think are cheap and remodeling them. But the area is still very much in the upswing between two worlds. There may be a house that has recently been fixed up that looks beautiful on one side of the street with a completely dilapidated neighborhood, renting for thousands of dollars a month, on the other.

Something tells me that Colby and Meredith are probably living on that side.

Prior to letting her go I ask Franny for all of Madison's social media information so I can look stuff up and get additional input from the computer tech guy who helps us do all the searches. Armed with a master's degree in Information Technology, Dax Utter has set up a lot of sting operations to help our department catch sex predators in the act before they actually hurt any kids.

It has brought a lot of positive attention to the department from the public and the media, helping us stop crimes before they are committed. For a while there, I worked as a decoy in a number of operations. My job consisted of texting and flirting with so-called upstanding members of our community who led secret double lives on the internet talking to underage girls and boys.

Prior to her leaving, I reassure Franny that I'll do my best to try to get to the bottom of this. I can't quite tell if she believes me or not, but I reassure her that I will.

5

CHARLOTTE

L ater that afternoon, while I'm catching up on the piles of paperwork, I run into Will on his way back from court. He looks worn out and blitzed, popping three liquid gels of Advil into his mouth. I fill him in on Franny's missing sister.

"Listen, I'd love to hear more, but I'm just really exhausted. The defense attorney grilled me about everything and I nearly tripped up. My head is pounding. Let's talk about this later," he says, plopping down behind his desk and closing his eyes for a moment.

I return my gaze to my computer and then look out the window. A crow jumps up and down on the grass outside. It's mid-spring, which is a glorious time in the desert.

Flowers are in bloom.

The days are longer, warm like summer elsewhere. There isn't a smidge of humidity and the air is crisp and dry, just like always, but it's not hot yet. There're no furnace winds. And after work, I decide to head out to the hills for a hike.

In another two months, five o'clock is going to be the hottest time of the day with temperatures well over 110 degrees Fahrenheit, occasionally sneaking into the 120s. But right now it's hovering just over the mid-90s.

The Indian Reservation is just a twenty minute drive from the station and that's where some of the best hiking trails are around here. I head to Palm Canyon, which is about five miles into the desert. It's a large canyon surrounded by hills with palm trees and a little creek and oasis in the middle. You can take the trail all around the rim or you can head down into the canyon down the steep slope, which is what I choose.

I have my water bottle with me and I regret forgetting the camelback at home. I decide to go for a short three mile hike to clear my head. The creek is filled, runs fast, and gathers in the small pools of water heading to the waterfall on the other side. There are a few people walking by and I nod hello to them scrambling up the boulders.

The last time I was here I saw a group of bighorn sheep looking over their domain. It's a rare sight in the middle of the day for them to make themselves so visible, a privilege that I won't soon forget.

At first, I listen to music then an audiobook to take my mind elsewhere, but then I pop the earphones out and just walk, enjoying the wild.

My thoughts inevitably return to Franny Dillard. It's highly unusual for a teenager to report her sister missing without her parents' approval. I have stepsisters through my father's second marriage and I can't imagine doing something like that at that age. But her concerns are real and require more investigation.

Perhaps something did happen to Madison and her parents are being too lax. From what I heard from Franny, her mother seems to have done a number of wild things as a teenager, but that doesn't mean that her daughter's anything like her.

It's hard when you see kids and teens to not compare their experience to your own, but in my line of work I've seen enough to know that people are quite different and they each live very different lives.

There are girls who have babies at that age, endure sexual assaults by family members for years, live in constant fear and darkness. Something that I could never imagine. My own life has been filled with some struggles, but I did have a loving father who cared about me, cared almost a little bit too much by being too involved in my life, or so I thought.

I have dinner with him next week, which I'm dreading again. It's not that I don't enjoy spending time with him. It's just that he puts a lot of pressure on me to be like him, to live up to his expectations.

And he still can't get over the fact that I don't work for the FBI. He's getting his lifetime achievement award as an Associate Director of the FBI. The awards ceremony got postponed a couple of months ago and now it's going to be in the summer. I'm supposed to give a speech or at least say something meaningful. Another thing that I'm dreading about it, besides going to D.C., and him talking me up to all his colleagues in hopes that they give me a job.

It has always been quite a disappointment to him that I did not pursue his line of work, but I have my reasons for doing that. It's something I've never shared with anyone and something that I will probably face this weekend. That is if I go to the reunion.

It's funny how thoughts come and go in your mind. The smallest thing can trigger an emotion and a memory. And then you can go for years hardly thinking about this terrible thing at all.

My twentieth anniversary of my eighth grade graduation is coming up this weekend. An old friend from all those years back is organizing it and made it clear on a couple of occasions that I should really attend. I can make up an excuse of course, work always is a good one, but something is pulling me back.

Perhaps it's time to make amends for what happened back then, back when I was thirteen years old, and the secret that we kept all of these years.

I don't want to go.

Don't get me wrong, it's probably the last place I want to be. But recently it has been this dark cloud over my head.

Clara Foster is organizing this informal reunion at her place in Long Beach. Probably the location where I had my most formative years. Other than that, I've changed schools more times than I can count.

My dad thought nothing of moving me around to follow his career promotions and changes. But it's in Long Beach, California, that I had this solid group of friends; four girls with whom I was very close.

We did everything together. We laughed, we cried, we slept over at each other's houses. Some of us were closer to each other than others, but we were all besties.

When I get closer and closer to the waterfall, I can hear it in the distance. It is not huge, but it's a couple of stories high and falls straight into a crystal blue lake. Underneath there are boulders, green grass sprouting nearby, as well as desert shrubs. Even though it's only been about a mile, I'm sweating in the ninety degree heat and my feet are on fire. I imagine the relief of slipping off my sneakers and putting my feet into the water.

Just then I hear them, their voices are getting louder with every moment.

"You stay away from me!" the woman yells.

"Who do you think you are?" the man asks.

For a moment I'm tempted to turn back, but I pick up the pace instead. Around the bend I see them.

He's grabbing her arm.

She's trying to get away.

They're both dressed in hiking gear and there's a backpack on the ground. A large one, the kind that you camp with rather than bring for the day.

"I don't need this!" she yells. "I don't need you in my life!"

"Yes, you do. Who do you think owns the van?" he snaps, pulling harder on her hand. She falls into him and then he grabs her by the throat.

"Hey!" I yell, my voice projecting around the walls of the canyon. "What do you think you're doing?"

"Get the hell out of here!" the man yells in my direction.

He's white, in his mid-twenties, sturdy, but thin, with the body of a long distance runner. If the woman's over eighteen, I'd be surprised. She has long blonde hair, wide set eyes, and she's undoubtedly beautiful.

"Get your hands off her right now. You're talking to a police officer."

The guy pulls away and furrows his brow.

"Oh, yeah? Show me some ID!" he snaps.

I reach for my weapon, but realize that I left the belt back in the office. I'm off duty now and I don't have the habit of carrying a weapon on me like some do, especially when I'm hiking. But I do have my identification.

"What's going on here?" I ask the woman.

She begins to sob. "I'm just trying to... He's my boyfriend. And we're just arguing. It's nothing."

"Oh, yeah? Is that why he has his hands around your throat?"

"Sometimes things just get out of hand. I don't think that we can afford to stay. He wants to stay in the van tonight again. And I'm tired of it. It's not as great as I thought it would be."

"Excuse me?" I ask.

"We can't afford to stay at a motel," the man snaps. "There's no point in wasting $70 on that and we probably can't even get one for $70. It'll be over a hundred. That would be the last of our money. How stupid can you be?"

"Can you please stop talking to her?" I say. "Go over there."

I separate them, sending him to one side of the waterfall and hating the fact that once again, something that is supposed to be a relaxing evening has turned into a work thing.

But at the same time, I'm glad that I'm here. I'm glad that I could solve this problem and deescalate the situation.

The woman and I talk, I find out that she's barely twenty and that she and her boyfriend have been living in this van trying to start a YouTube and Instagram channel, but things have gotten kind of hard. They don't have much money and it's hard to make pretty aspirational pictures about how wonderful your life is when you're broke and trying to save every last penny.

"I just really need a break," she tells me. "I know that we can't really afford it, but I can call my mom and ask her to send me some more money."

"And what's she going to say about me? Huh, Madison?" the man snaps.

I pause for a moment, holding my breath. Can this be her? She fits the description but her hair is long and light.

"Madison? Is that your name?" I whisper. "Madison Dillard."

She stares at me blankly when I say Dillard.

"Nyland," she says. "I'm Madison Nyland. He's Michael Peritte. Yeah, my mom's going to give us the money and she'll tell me that I have to come back home and that I shouldn't be wasting my time living in this van and starting this blog. But I want to do this with you, Michael. Don't you see? And you're just making it so difficult and impossible."

Even though they're separated, they're now arguing loudly with each other across the water.

"I'm sorry. I hate to bother you," Madison says. "I don't mean to interrupt your hike. This whole thing has just gotten so out of control."

"No matter what, he has no right to put his hands on you. Let alone around your throat. Do you want to press charges?"

"No, I don't."

"I really want you to reconsider that, Madison. What he's doing is being abusive. He's trying to control you."

"No, it's just the fight. It means nothing."

"But it does. You can have a disagreement, but he has no right to do that."

"I love him," she says. "We're great together except for things have been kind of tense. I think it's just because we have money problems, that's it. And he's right. We shouldn't stay in a hotel. I was just getting sick of being in that van. There's no air conditioning. It's really hot. And it's just too much. Sometimes you want to get away. Do you know what that's like?"

I nod.

"More than you know," I say after a long pause. Even though she decides not to press charges, I cut my hike short and walk them both back to their van.

Tempers seem to have simmered down for now.

But I wonder how they'll act back inside? She refused to press charges and well, I could have made it more of a thing since I was a witness, but if she refuses to cooperate, there are limitations to what I can do as a law enforcement officer.

As I watch them climb into the van and pull out of the parking lot, I hope that this is the worst of it. I hope that it doesn't get worse.

6

CHARLOTTE

On the way back from the canyon I make plans for dinner, something healthy, full of antioxidants, perhaps a pre-made arugula salad that I have in the refrigerator.

I'm not much of a cook but I've been eating nothing but fried food and junk food, lots of takeout over the last couple of weeks. And it is not only catching up to me, but it's also making me feel sluggish and annoyed. I've stocked up on plenty of salads with dressing, with minimal processed ingredients, and I hope to focus more on my health in the coming weeks and months.

That was part of the reason for going on the hike. I went on one yesterday as well and if I can build up a little bit more of this habit, I know that it's going to serve me well.

Just as I pull up to my garage, my phone rings. I'm tempted to let it go to voice mail, but I recognize the number from when she wrote it down for me earlier.

It's Franny, perhaps she's calling with good news.

"Hey, what's up?" I answer.

"Is she there? Did she come back?" Franny takes a big gulp of air and I can hear her struggling for breath.

"Are you okay, Franny?"

"No," she says through a sob. "No, no, they're dead. They're both dead."

She starts to say something else that I don't comprehend.

"Franny, you have to calm down. I can't understand you."

"Come, come here, please. They're dead. My parents are dead." I make out through the sobs.

"What do you mean? Did you call the police?"

"*You* are the police. I'm calling you."

"Okay. Stay on the line," I say as I enter her address into my car's navigation. "Don't touch anything and just stay where you are, okay?"

I put her on hold and call the station, asking for backup. I don't know the details of anything, but perhaps a deputy can get there before I can.

When I return, I tell her to stay put.

"It's going to take me half an hour to get there, Franny. But maybe somebody will get there earlier."

"I have to go," she says. "I can't..."

"Franny, I'm here for you. Stay on the line for me please."

"Okay," she says, sobbing.

"You don't have to say anything, just stay there so I know that you're there and you're safe."

"There's no one here," she says.

"Have you been inside the house?"

"No."

"Okay. Don't go in."

As I drive over, I expect her to stay on the line, but a few minutes later she hangs up. I don't know if we're getting disconnected or not. I try to call her back, but no one answers.

I say a silent prayer that nothing bad happened, that she's okay. But I won't know either way. I go through a few yellow lights, drive fifteen miles over the speed limit and shave off ten minutes from the drive.

When I arrive, luckily I see two patrol cars parked around the gates.

Directions take me on a dirt road.

Past the open gate, I follow the dirt road to the house out in the distance. It's in the middle of the desert, nothing for miles but shrubs and a few palm trees.

Greenwald and Dockerson are there. Franny is sitting on a big rock holding the leash of a dog who yaps in our direction. Greenwald asks her to put the dog away somewhere so that we can talk and she bursts into tears.

She's dressed in the same *Little House on the Prairie* dress and her shoulders move up and down under the exaggerated shoulder sleeves.

"Franny." I walk up to her.

She sees me and immediately rushes to me, wrapping her arms around me.

"Do you know her?" Greenwald mouths in my direction. I give him a slight nod.

"Franny, tell me what's going on."

She shakes her head and pulls away from me. Her dog's leash is still in her hand. I realize that the Australian Shepherd is more of a yapper than a doer, but it's still very distracting.

"Franny, we have to talk to you. Can you get your dog to be quiet in any way, or you'll have to put him inside."

She pets the dog on top of his head and tells him to sit down. Much to my surprise, he listens.

"He's just being protective," she says. "Yes. I understand. My parents are over there," she says, pointing to the car in front of the house.

It's a one story double wide style trailer with parking right outside, no garage in sight.

I leave her for a few minutes and tell her that I'm going to take a look at the scene, which the deputies have already taped off.

Greenwald follows me while Dockerson stays behind with Franny. Luckily the dog stops barking long enough for me to think.

The old, beige Cadillac is parked up front.

Next to it, I see the bodies.

7

CHARLOTTE

I walk on some of the softest sand I've ever stood on, desert silt, until I get to the driveway. Parts of it are desert silt while others are uneven, rocky ground, packed down, hard, rocky terrain.

When Franny said that her family wanted to move and have a little bit of land, they weren't kidding. This is only thirty minutes away from town and it's like another world. The property is dotted with creosote bushes, palm trees, and the occasional crooked Joshua tree.

Franny's parents are lying on the ground next to the Cadillac. The closer I get to them, the further away her sobs get and the more I'm able to focus.

Franny's father, a man in his mid-forties, lies on his stomach, head down in the packed sand, just to one side of the rocky driveway. His body is right next to the driver's door.

The front door of the Cadillac is open. It looks like he was shot in the back through the shoulder blades and fell right there.

There's blood on the side of the car from where Jennifer fell and tried to grab a hold of it for support. It looks like she was shot in the stomach first, then tried to prop herself up with the door by grabbing onto it, perhaps shutting it, before she was shot again. She was shot in the stomach and then again in the chest.

I don't want to touch the bodies. I don't have gloves. But when the forensics people arrive, they'll let us know whether they're cold to the touch.

I walk around and make sure that the area is properly taped off, following all procedures.

While we wait, I return to Franny, sit down on the boulder next to her, and look at the way the wind makes little ridges in the soft sand underneath our feet. I went scuba diving once and it reminds me of the ridges you see the water make underwater.

Franny's holding a stick and drawing something on the ground, connecting one dot to another in no particular pattern. Tears are still running down her cheeks, but now she seems more dazed than anything else.

"Can you tell me what happened?" I ask.

"I don't know," she says, shaking her head.

When she looks up and sees the bodies, she covers her mouth and begins to sob. I turn her physically around to face the entrance and the gate leading to her property with her back toward her dead parents.

"Talk to me. Please."

"I just came home and they were like this." She shakes her head in disbelief.

Her eyes are bloodshot, full of terror. Her nose is red and a little bulbous. The sleeve of her hoodie, which she wasn't wearing earlier in the day, is drenched.

"What did you do after you came to the police station?" I ask. "Did you come back here? Did you do something else?"

"I went to the art museum with my grandmother," she says with a shrug. "She knew Mom and Dad were working long hours and they were busy, and there's a free day at the museum so we did that.

Walked around, got some coffee, talked about Madison. And then I came here. That's it."

"That's it?" I ask. "And how did you get here after the museum?"

"Grandma dropped me off down the street. I needed to pick up the mail and she needed to get to class so I was just going to walk up the driveway."

I look back. If this is true, her grandmother would have been able to see the dead bodies from down the hill where the mailbox was located.

"Yeah. I had some homework to do, and I thought I would help Mom with dinner. I was going to maybe try to cook this new recipe that I found online."

"Do you usually cook dinner?"

"No, but I've been getting more into it. My parents order a lot of takeout or just pre-made things and I'm getting sick of it, so I decided to teach myself how to cook."

I nod, looking at the hoodie again. There's nothing unusual about it, per se, except that if she wasn't inside since she talked to me, where did it come from?

"Is this your hoodie?" I ask, trying to be as casual as possible.

She looks up at me, a little bit surprised.

"No, it's my grandmother's," she mumbles, inhaling and trying to get her nose to stop running. "The museum is really cold, so Grandma always carries extra clothes, sweaters and stuff in her car. She lent it to me. Why does that matter?"

"Just wondering. Just trying to understand exactly what happened."

"Look, I wasn't here. I don't know what you want me to say," she says after a quick look at me, probably suspecting that I'm suspecting that there's more to the story than she's saying.

"I wasn't home. They were supposed to be working today. And it's Saturday and I had nothing to do."

"Do you do any sports or activities?" I ask.

"Yeah, I was volunteering at the hospital for a while, but I'm off now," she says. "I needed more time to study so that I don't fall behind in school."

I nod, making a note in my journal that I need to talk to people at the hospital, as well as her grandmother, and check with the art museum to confirm her alibi.

This is all procedure, of course. In reality, I don't suspect her in the least.

At sixteen years old, as innocent as she looks, and as concerned as she was about her sister, and now this? These tears, this level of emotion, this would be quite an act.

And to execute her parents like that? I don't know.

I've seen some dark things in my life, but this would be some of the darkest if she had anything to do with it.

Still, I have to follow procedure because many cops and investigators have gotten in plenty of trouble just following their guts, making excuses for people that they should not excuse, siding with criminals.

"So your parents were working at home? You said they have an office here?"

"Yeah, they have an office in town, but they do a lot of their work at home on weekends, just because it is a bit of a drive and there's really no reason to be there. And here they can do some stuff on the farm when they take breaks."

"And how has business been going?" I ask.

"From what I hear, pretty well. They got a bunch of new clients, but it's been stressful since some of their business clients have audits with the IRS."

"Taxes were due April fifteenth," I point out. "Has that been stressful for them in any way?"

"Yes, of course. It's always crunch time around that time. But a number of clients got their taxes postponed, but some are getting audited. I don't know who. And so they were sort of stressing about that. Do you think that this was someone that they worked with?" Franny asks.

I shake my head. "I have no idea. We're going to do everything in our power to investigate and talk to everyone."

"I just don't know who would want them killed. I mean, and for what? They're just accountants. They're just normal people and I just can't imagine," she says, beginning to cry again.

She puts her head in her lap, hanging her shoulders, and I wrap my arm around hers. This girl has been through a lot. And perhaps I'm taking certain liberties with my professionalism, but she needs a friend right now.

As I sit here and wait, I know that we only have a few minutes before this crime scene comes to life.

Out in the distance, I see the forensics team pulling up, driving on the unpaved road. The two deputies have already set up tables and tents for us to do our work.

A double homicide is not a common thing in this town, especially one of two upstanding citizens.

We're going to be scrutinized for how we conduct this work, and my career can be staked on it.

When Lieutenant Soderman's car pulls up, I know it's about to begin.

8

CHARLOTTE

While I fill in the lieutenant about what I know so far, Deputy Greenwald calls Franny's grandmother, who should be here shortly.

We walk around the scene as the forensics team starts to collect evidence. Lieutenant Soderman is a heavyset guy in his fifties who prefers to stay in the office and deal with paperwork. He rose up the ranks a while ago when things were a little different. But then again, there're not that many police officers that like paperwork, and so if you find one who does and who enjoys engaging in all the politics of the department, that's going to be the one who goes further careerwise.

When I was just a patrol officer, it was he who advised me about how to play by the rules better, so

I could become a detective.

I used to go to work, come back, and just put in my hours. I didn't do anything beyond that and it hurt me.

It wasn't until Lieutenant Soderman, at that time Sergeant, sat me down and explained it all to me over lunch. He said that I was a good cop, but I was selling myself short just doing patrols. That's when I realized that I had to step it up.

"This is a career path," the lieutenant said. "If you want to make detective, get the good hours, the regular 9 to 5, get paid overtime for any outside work; you've got to play by the rules. You have to socialize with other cops, make friends. At least, be seen and remembered."

It took a couple of rounds after I finally figured it out and realized that I didn't just want to be a patrol deputy anymore with way too many hours and a lot less pay. I passed the written test and seemed to do pretty well on the interview portion of the exam. But there were all these additional points assigned by a committee. And if those people don't know you well, you're going to get passed over.

We walk around the crime scene, looking at the dead bodies that are slowly getting processed. It never happens as fast as it does in the movies.

Forensics can take weeks, usually months to process, and that's for a case that's sent to the private lab. If it's not a high priority situation, DNA results can sit and linger for months, if not years at the state labs, which don't require extra fees.

Everything comes at a price. You want something done faster, it costs more, and the case has to be prioritized over other cases.

"Seems like this is going to be something newsworthy," the lieutenant says, going back to his car and grabbing a baseball hat to put over his balding head.

He looks a little bit younger now. More hip, even.

Like someone who does this often, but the dressy clothes and his suit give him an air of authority that I don't have.

"The news media's going to be here soon," the lieutenant says. "We haven't had a double homicide like this in a while. If ever."

"Yeah, this isn't a drug case. Unlikely. Two upstanding citizens of the community. This is definitely going to make the news."

"Well, I just hope not national," the lieutenant says.

"That could be good, too," I point out. "More publicity."

"Only if we solve it. If not, you know what happens. They make a mockery out of everything we do here. Those true crime shows put on their so-called experts without any experience in the field, and they second-guess us. "Should we have done this? No, we *should* have done that."

To say that the lieutenant is not a fan of the true crime phase that's currently ruling television, podcast, and YouTube land would be a massive understatement.

"Back in the day, there used to just be *Dateline*, and that's it," he says. "Maybe *20/20*. But they just focused on O.J. Simpson, Caylee Anthony, or Scott Peterson. Now it seems like they're trying to bring up all sorts of old cases."

"But you can't deny the fact that all the new interests and the web-sleuthing can actually bring attention to and solve some of these cases, right?" I point out.

He shrugs.

"They definitely bring attention, but that's about it. In terms of solving cases, it's still good old police work and investigations. Nothing else."

I don't want to argue about this with him. I'm well aware of his opinions, and they largely conflict with mine. Personally I think that there can be a lot of good done by independent investigators. Detectives can sometimes be very narrow-minded in their approach, and I've made this opinion clear, but he also doesn't want to hear it.

He walks around the crime scene, looking carefully at the ground. I know what he's looking for. Stray bullets, casings, anything else that we could collect.

"It seems like the shots came from pretty close up," I say. "I don't see any bullets or ejected shell casings but maybe they will be able to find something with a closer investigation."

"What about tire marks?" he asks.

I shrug. "You can see in the driveway as good as me. The gravel and the uneven road make it hard to tell if anyone was here. I don't know whether they have any cameras set up, but maybe."

I walk a little bit closer to the house.

"I didn't want *her* to go in," I say. "Deputies looked inside and secured the perimeter. But I haven't been in."

"Did you ask the girl?" I look in Franny's direction.

She continues to cry with her head buried in her legs in a fetal position. Dockerson with his army crew cut stands next to her, clearly uncomfortable with all of the emotions.

"I didn't ask her about the cameras yet. I figured we'd have time to get to that, but as you can see, if there are any, none of them are visible."

"Ah, this looks like a case for forensics and will likely require a lot of interviewing and digging into their past."

"Yeah, they have a tax accountancy with a number of clients. It could be related to that," I say.

"Hope you like numbers, Pierce. And if you don't, you're going to brush up on all of that. That's a lot of paperwork to go through."

"Yeah. We'll just see where the evidence leads us," I say, and he gives me an approving nod.

"I think I found something, Detective!" one of the CSI guys yells, waving me over.

Franny looks up excited but I wave to Dockerson to keep her away.

"The man's teeth were pulled," the forensic guy says.

Cold sweat runs down my spine.

"The wife's, too."

9

CHARLOTTE

Franny's grandmother arrives a little bit later, frazzled and overwhelmed. I try to make a mental note of what she looks like but my thoughts keep drifting back to the missing teeth.

Why would someone kill them and take their teeth?

The grandmother has dark short hair, probably in her late sixties but could easily pass for fifty-five. She's trim, but casually dressed: a sweatshirt and loose jeans from Costco.

She pulls up in a Toyota Corolla and runs over to Franny, pulling her into her arms, without bothering to close the door.

For a moment, I find this peculiar because I'm not one to ever leave the car door open, but I know that others are. Does Franny's mother have this tendency? Is it even relevant?

She holds her granddaughter for a little while and I give her some space. A few minutes later, with her arms firmly around Franny, she looks up at me and asks, "What's wrong? What happened?"

I'm keenly aware of the fact that Franny's parents are right over my shoulder. She glances over, but she stays composed. Tears well up in her eyes, but she doesn't break down. She's here to be strong for her granddaughter, and I appreciate that.

"Franny said that she walked to the police station and made a statement about her sister today. Is that right?" Doran asks.

I nod. I call her Mrs. Dillard once, but she shakes her head and insists on Pamela, which is fine by me.

"What did you do today, Pamela?" I ask.

"Woke up, had breakfast, went on a walk, did some yoga, then met up with my granddaughter."

"And where did you pick her up from?" I ask.

"She took the bus from the police station. Though she only told me that afterward. She met me at the art museum." Pamela says. "She doesn't drive yet. She's too scared."

I give a knowing sigh.

"And you went to what museum?"

"The one by the Palm Oasis. Modern Art. They had a free day today and we needed to spend some time together. I know that she'd been very worried about her sister. And finally, when we were having lunch there, she broke down and told me that she'd made a report."

"Did you think that was… appropriate?" I ask, searching for the right word.

She nods.

"It's been three weeks. I don't know what's going on. And I'm worried about my granddaughter. Her parents didn't seem to be too concerned. And now this. Why would this happen?" She looks over my shoulder and begins to cry.

I start to ask her a few more questions, but I need to give her a second first. These moments are so full of energy, and it took me a long time in my career to figure out how to read people correctly.

When to step in and push, when to pull back. I still don't know. And I wonder if it's a skill that takes years to hone.

A little bit later, I ask Pamela once again about her day. She repeats her story, mentioning yoga first, then the walk. I try to throw her off a little by asking her what she had for breakfast. It's a strategy to try to get the interviewee to mess up.

Sometimes a person will tell a story in different ways, and you can catch them in a lie.

Other times they repeat it word for word, which is also a little concerning since you would never tell the same story in the exact same way.

But all of these are just hints as to what could have happened and what is true and what isn't.

We all know that you can't judge people by their grief or lack of it. And that there are different ways to react to the loss of a child, a parent, or a friend.

For now, I'm just gathering information.

A FEW HOURS LATER, I'm running late.

I check the time and drive to the bar a little bit too fast. I hate being late. I have a plan to meet up with Will and now I'm regretting scheduling it. But after a whole afternoon and evening of police work, I need a drink and just time to clear my head.

"You have no idea what kind of case you got landed in my lap," I say, walking into the Red

Horseshoe, a western-themed bar that has recently become something of a cop hangout in this part of town. It has wood paneling all around, all signs pointing to a dive bar, but the cocktails are quite elevated, and expensive to match, but the beers are cheap.

Will is already sitting on a stool, saving me a spot. The place is getting busy. I fill him in on the details and he laughs. He's been off for a number of hours, but I came straight here.

"So that's what I'm dealing with, and I have to go to Long Beach soon."

"Don't worry about it. I mean, it's a big case. You should be glad," he says.

I shrug, taking a swig of the beer. I'm not a big fan, but I like that it's affordable.

"Can you believe it? I mean, the girl just came in to make a statement about her missing sister, and now her parents are dead with their freaking teeth pulled! Like, what the heck is going on?"

"You think she had anything to do with it?"

"I highly doubt it," I say. "That would have been one hell of a performance. But who knows nowadays. Her alibi does check out, and I doubt that she worked with her grandmother to kill her own father and mother. I mean, what's the point of that?"

"Property? Money? Greed? Pick a motive."

"I know, I know. You're the cynic," I say.

"Listen, I told you that I had time to hang out tonight, but something's come up."

"Oh, yeah?" I raise one eyebrow. "What, like a date?"

"Kind of. Erin and I-"

"Shh!" I put my finger over my lips.

"It's kind of the anniversary of the day that we first met all of those years ago. I forgot, and she had this whole thing planned."

I shake my head with disapproval. "How is she doing?"

"As well as can be expected. Working at that law firm with her friend, putting in lots of hours. She doesn't have any cases going to trial or anything, but she said that if all goes well, they'll have something like that for her next year, so she's excited."

"That's good. I'm glad that things are improving for her," I say.

"But?" Will puts words in my mouth.

"But you know what I'm worried about."

He shrugs and looks down at the condensation on the outside of his bottle. "You shouldn't worry about that," he says.

"Really? Because I have a feeling that they have enough on you to fire you without a pension. Maybe even prosecute you. That's something that I shouldn't worry about?"

"I don't know," he says. "I mean, of course I worry, but I love her. Always have."

"I know, and I'm really happy for you two," I say. "But you have to take it easy. You don't want people to find out, and this is kind of a small town. Someone might see you out with her. Her case was front page news."

"We could have started dating afterward, after she was cleared of the double murder."

"Yes, but you didn't. And who knows? Maybe besides me, someone else finds something out. It's just I want you to be more careful. It's not just your career that's on the line."

"I know," Will says. "I know. I would hate myself if anything happened to you."

"I am covering up for you. This should have gone to Internal Affairs and you should have been off that case."

"But I needed to prove her innocence," Will pleads. "I knew that she had nothing to do with the murder of her ex-husband and his wife."

"Okay, and now that you have, you still have to take it easy. You have to figure out some other way, some other storyline of how you met, how all this happened. Ideally, it would include nothing about your past with her all of those years ago."

"Okay." He nods.

We sit for a few minutes as he says that he's not meeting up with her for a little while longer. I feel like our get-together has a time clock, and I'd rather be home at this point, but it's fine.

I'm fine.

He has another couple of drinks while I continue to nurse my one bottle. I'm not much of a lush. Anything but that, really.

This is enough for me to relax and unwind. And then just as Will's about to leave, somebody walks up to him.

"Dylan?" Will says, a big grin spreading across his face. He stands up and gives him a warm hug. "What are you doing here?"

"I live here now. Been here about six months."

A tall, dark stranger shakes my hand and Will introduces him as Dylan Ferreira.

"Dylan and I met in some training a long time ago. He was a cop in San Francisco. Detective, actually."

"Yeah. Got a raise." He laughs as he looks me up and down in that way that people do when they consider whether or not they want to ask you out.

"So you're here? I didn't realize you were at the department. You're working for the county?"

"No. I'm actually a firefighter now." Dylan smiles, his pearly whites blinding me.

"Seriously?"

Dylan nods. "Yeah. Police work got too much for me, but I like the benefits and the retirement plan, so…"

"You decided to be a firefighter?" Will can't get over this fact. "Do you remember how much we used to make fun of them?"

"Yeah, running into burning buildings, stopping wildfires…"

"Rescuing cats?" Will adds, and we all chuckle at Dylan's expense, but he seems to be a good sport about it. Will isn't being mean-spirited.

They catch up a little bit and I nod along, staying busy with my phone. And then all of a sudden, Will looks at the time and says that he has to go.

"Sorry about that, but give me your number. I really want to catch up, for real."

And just like that, Dylan and I are left alone.

10

CHARLOTTE

I'm about to leave, but I decided to stick around and talk to Dylan a little bit longer. He offers to buy me another drink, but I insist on getting it myself.

"So, you and Will work together?" he asks.

"Yes, we do." I nod.

"What's he like as a partner?"

"It's not exactly partnership work. We work some cases together, some cases separately. It's a small department so wherever they have a need that's where we end up going.

I take a sip of my beer. It's a good default beverage when you don't want to get too buzzed. "So what brought you all the way here?

You worked for San Francisco as a detective, right?"

"Yeah."

When Dylan nods, his hair falls on his face. It's dark and full and cut a little above the ears.

"Let's just say I had a few issues so I decided to take a break to do something else."

He's avoiding the question, not saying anything directly, and I can appreciate that.

"We have something in common. I used to work for the LAPD. Rampart Division."

"Rampart?" He raises an eyebrow.

"Yeah. Doesn't have the best reputation, does it?" I laugh.

"Didn't they shut it all down? Because the cops themselves were dealing drugs."

I nod.

"Yeah, that was a little bit before my time. But things changed only slightly after the authorities got involved."

"Well, it's hard for the police to police themselves, isn't it? Thin Blue Line and everything."

I nod and take another sip.

I let the silence between us linger and it feels strangely comfortable. Dylan's dressed in a casual button down shirt and gray pants. His broad shoulders wrap around his slim frame and he has blue eyes that won't let mine leave his face.

He makes me feel strangely at peace and yet worried all at the same time, anxious but in a good way. Nervous, perhaps.

"So tell me something about you," I say.

"What would you like to know?"

"Tell me something you enjoy."

"I like fighting fires."

"You do?" I ask.

"Yeah. After I quit the force I wasn't sure what to do but decided to pursue firefighting. It felt sort of nice to help people in that real way. It's the same thing that made me pursue law enforcement in the first place. But with a lot less politics."

I pick at a groove in the counter. It's deep and thick, like it was made by a switchblade.

"A house or a forest is on fire," Dylan continues. "You go there and do your job. You put it out. It really feels like there's only one thing to do and it's the right thing."

"It wasn't like that to be a cop?" I ask.

"After a number of years in San Francisco, I felt like I was really skirting the law."

"Was there a lot of corruption?"

"No, not in my department, but it was complicated. There were pressures from the government, city officials, residents, the technocrats. Everybody wanted something and they wanted us to enforce it for them. We were suddenly supposed to deal with not only murders and theft but also homeless encampments, housing disputes, anything and everything."

"That's one of the reasons I moved out here," I say.

"Oh, really?"

"Yeah. The big city police force was just too much for me. After a while, I couldn't deal with it. I didn't want to go to murder scene after murder scene and have them go unsolved anymore. I was tired of the suicide and overdose calls. I wanted to help people, too, but I also wanted to have a life."

"So, since you're a detective, you work regular hours?" Dylan asks.

"Yeah, much better than when I was on patrol. You just clock in and clock out and everything else is overtime. Unless we have a big case. Like now."

"What happened?"

"A sixteen-year-old girl reported her older sister missing. She's been gone for three weeks. She's probably a runaway and it didn't seem like the parents were very concerned. After making the report, the girl went home and found both of her parents murdered in the driveway."

"Wow, that really sucks," Dylan says.

"Yeah, it's not ideal," I joke, trying to make light of a terrible situation.

"Do you have any idea who did it? Any leads?"

I shake my head no.

"I was just beginning the investigation today. The girl's in shock, obviously. She's staying at her grandparents' and I'm going to talk to them tomorrow morning."

A moment of silence passes between us. It's comfortable once again. Dylan looks at me in that way that I know that he likes what he sees.

I lick my lips and he smiles.

"So, are you here on a permanent basis?" I ask.

"Yep." He nods. "The hours in Mesquite County are good so far, but the summers and fall are obviously busy. Fire season, you know. They can send us anywhere around Southern California and even up north, depending on the situation."

Fire season is not an easy time around here.

Mesquite County is all desert in the valley, dry creosote bushes with little precipitation, and heavily forested mountains.

The two places are only an hour or so away from each other, but are starkly different. In the winters, the temperatures hover around the mid-seventies on the desert floor and drop down to the twenties and thirties with heavy snowfall up in the mountains.

"That's good," I say shyly.

Dylan smiles at me. He has dimples in his cheeks making him irresistible.

"I was kind of wondering what your schedule was as well. Maybe I can take you out on a date sometime. A proper one."

I prop my head up with my hand and look him up and down.

"How do you know that *I'm* not married?" I ask.

"I don't. Are you?"

"How do I know that *you're* not?" I ask.

"I'm divorced. It was finalized two years ago and it prompted me to change careers. My life kind of collapsed at that time. I came here to start something new. There was an opening and it sounded nice. Seventy degrees and sunny for nine months out of the year. I was tired of the overcast skies and the constant drizzle of gray San Francisco."

"I heard it's green there," I say. "Lush."

"Yeah, but I got ficus trees all around my pool and I can swim in it year round."

Is he really this charming? I wonder and smile at him, finishing the last of my beer.

"So, what do you think?" Dylan asks. "Can I take you out sometime? Pick you up? Make it an official date?"

I stare deep into his eyes. "Yes, I'd like that," I say after a little bit of a pause.

Watching him lick his lips, it takes everything within me not to kiss him.

11

CHARLOTTE

The following morning, I pack a bag for the weekend. Casual clothes, jeans, nice blouses, a pair of boots, and sneakers, nothing fancy, a couple of hoodies and sweaters as well since it can get a little bit chilly there in the wintertime.

After talking to Franny and her grandparents, I'm going to go to the reunion in Long Beach. It starts tonight at six, but I'm planning on coming back on Sunday. I don't know if I'm going to meet up with any of my old friends on Saturday, but it's nice having the day off anyway.

I pack my makeup bag and look at myself in the mirror, feeling nervous and uncertain about what is in store for me. I should just probably leave everything as it is; certain secrets, perhaps, should be taken to the grave. But I know that we did something wrong, not telling anyone about what happened, and perhaps it's time to make amends. Certain people need to know the truth.

Is that why this reunion is happening in the first place? I have no idea what Clara's after, but she was insistent on me coming even when I tried to get out of it. I haven't seen her in years, twenty to be exact, ever since we moved away the summer before ninth grade. I wasn't in touch, not in any substantial manner, with anyone back there. It's funny how time passes and there're certain people that you never forget about. Or perhaps you do and you give them no thought, and then suddenly they come back into your life and you wonder where they've been all this time. What have they been doing?

Clara Foster is one of those people. I know some of the details, of course. She has three kids, one is a teenager, the others are quite young. Two husbands. Still married to the second one.

Sometimes, when you go back in time, so to speak, you become the person that the other people remember you as. I like to think that I'm very different from the twelve-, thirteen-, fourteen-year-old version of me that they knew, but perhaps I'm not more confident or certain of who I am.

I was such a cynic back then, always expected the worst from everyone, partly because I tried to please my father, tried to get him to like me.

If I was more cynical than him, he would laugh and say, "Wow, I thought that I had it bad."

But if I ever said anything nice about anyone, ever looked at the bright side of something or someone's intentions, he would laugh and call me *naive*. That was perhaps the harshest thing and the meanest thing that he could call me.

My father is Associate Deputy Director of the FBI. His biggest disappointment is that I didn't follow him into that line of work. He has absolutely no respect for this department and, in fact, spends a lot of time mocking me for working here, for doing something below my station, for not living up to his expectations.

The thing about time is that you learn how to use it to your advantage. I can now confidently say that I don't care what he thinks and that I'm no longer seeking his approval. I wish, however, that we had a better relationship, but it seems impossible.

The directions on the GPS take me to a gated community called Mission Park. I enter the code and somebody at the other end opens the gate. This is the one without a guard, just a code and a visitor lane on one side and residents driving through on the other with transponders connected to their cars.

Mission Park is quite nice. I've been in a number of these communities, but unlike others, this one has sidewalks and nice manicured lawns. Some have desert landscaping, but others are still holding on to the old way of being, green grass all around, thick, beautiful, lush trees, and a mix of palm trees. I'm certain of the fact that there are no houses here under two thousand five hundred square feet and most are probably over three thousand with big backyards and pools.

The Dillard grandparents have a three-car garage and a small gate leading to a courtyard in front of their front door. The gate is open and when I knock on the door, Pamela answers promptly. She welcomes me into her beautiful home, a tall fourteen-foot ceiling and a formal living room looking onto the lush landscape out front greet me.

There are about forty yards of backyard grass and a trampoline that seems to be left over from the olden days, when the kids were still young and liked to jump.

Pamela's hair is neatly brushed and she's wearing a thick mask of makeup. But through it all, I notice the dark circles under her eyes, they are bloodshot. It has only been a day since she discovered that her son was brutally murdered along with his wife. I don't think it's been long enough for that news to sink in fully.

"My condolences again, for everything that has happened," I say as she points me to an arm chair in front of the fireplace and takes a seat on the couch across from me.

"I appreciate you saying that," she says, folding her hands neatly across her lap.

A few minutes later, Mr. Richard Dillard comes over and sits next to his wife. They're both in their sixties, or perhaps early seventies, but fit with plenty of sun on their skin. Like his wife, he insists that I do away with formalities and call him Richard.

There are pictures of Richard playing golf at various courses on the wall behind me. They are clearly staying active. Pamela looks like she could do a downward facing dog with more flexibility than I can even though she probably has thirty-five years on me.

"How's Franny doing?" I ask.

"She'll come out in a little bit," Richard says. "We just wanted to talk to you alone for now and let her rest. The doctor prescribed her some Valium to take the edge off. She couldn't stop crying last night."

"Yes, I understand," I say. "This has been an unimaginable tragedy. I want her to rest but the other reason I'm here is that I am concerned about Madison."

"Yes, we are, too. We wanted to talk to you about her as well," Richard says.

"A few hours before she found her parents dead, Franny came to the station to talk to me. She made a report. She wanted me to file a missing person's report for her sister."

"Yes, that's what she told her us," they say almost simultaneously.

"She also told me that her parents did not want this to happen, or weren't particularly interested in finding her."

Richard and Pamela exchange glances, and I look at them more closely.

"Can you tell me anything about that? Why wouldn't they be interested?"

"I think they thought that she just needed some time and that she'd be back. Things were kind of complicated for her," Pamela says. "She was a straight A student and she had her eyes set on UC Santa Barbara. That was her dream school. And she got in."

"She got in?" I ask.

"Yes, she did. She got into every school she applied for. It was very exciting."

"So what happened?" I ask. "Why did she go to Palm Valley Community College?"

"There's nothing wrong with that," Richard says.

"Of course not," I add quickly, embarrassed. "I didn't mean anything by it."

"You can get an excellent education at the junior colleges, but it was a very big step down for Madison," Richard says, running his hands through his salt and pepper hair. "She didn't belong there. The students there were older with kids and families of their own. She should have been in a dorm living on campus, hanging out with friends."

Pamela begins to cry, burying her head in her hands. The tragedy that this family has endured is insurmountable.

"I'm very sorry for both of you. I want you to know that," I say. This is what I don't like most about my job, being the one to comfort the victims.

"Of course, she started hanging out with the wrong crowd. I guess she met them at Desert Willow Country Club. I don't know," Pamela says.

"Were her parents unhappy about her friendships?" I ask.

"Not that I know of."

"Did she have a boyfriend?"

12

CHARLOTTE

My question seems to take Richard and Pamela by surprise. I clear my throat and ask again.

"Did Madison have a boyfriend?"

"Not that we know of. I think her parents were kind of embarrassed about what has been going on with her. They didn't tell us much," Pamela says. "One day we were celebrating her getting into Santa Barbara and the next it was like nothing happened. It was like everything had changed. She said that she wasn't going to go away to college. She said that she was going to keep living at home. And there was no explanation whatsoever."

"And you have no idea what happened?" I ask.

"No, they sort of told us as a matter of fact. When we pressed further, they said they didn't want to talk about it. That she needed space, that she needed to spend time at home."

"Do you think it was their initiative? Do you think they were stopping her from going, Richard?"

"I have no idea," he says. "We thought that at first, but then we met up with Michael and he said that he was very sad about everything. He said that something bad had happened at school and things were different now, but he couldn't say what it was. We never got to the bottom of it. We kept planning on talking to them, but we only met up in restaurants, public places, and it just didn't feel right to talk there. After a while we thought, well, maybe she can just go to school there for a year and transfer. But things got worse and worse. Her relationship with my son deteriorated, her relationship with her mother was basically nonexistent, and then she left."

"How?" I ask.

"She went to stay at her friend's house and she never came back. That's all we know."

"Did you ask them why they haven't made a police report?" I ask.

They nod.

"Of course. We were worried, but we also know our son and our daughter-in-law," Pamela says. "Jennifer did almost the exact same thing when she was a teenager. They met when Michael was driving cross country on his motorcycle. She's from upstate NY originally. Some little town that's not on any map. She waited on him at a diner. They went on a few dates while he was in town and then he asked her to ride away with him to California. And she did."

"She had a strained relationship with her parents when they met," Richard adds, "And it was love at first sight. She'd just graduated from high school and he was much older. He'd taken a trip across the country on his motorcycle and wanted to see the country."

"Was she in touch with her parents though?" I ask.

"Not much." They shake their heads. "But they weren't very nice people."

"Is this why they never reported Madison missing?" I ask. "Because they thought that she'd met a guy and went to sow her wild oats?"

Richard and Dora exchange looks.

"Please tell me, whatever it is," I insist. "I need your help to try to figure out what happened."

"Last year, I would have never thought that Madison would do anything like that," Pamela begins. "She was such a good girl. Straight A student. Workaholic. President of Student Council. She was a great sister and daughter. But this year she changed completely. She stopped coming by as much. She started to wear all black and do her makeup really heavy. I know that teenagers go through phases but this was more than that. Like something was really wrong."

"Michael and Jennifer think that the world is the same as it was back then," Richard says, using the present tense accidentally and then recoiling in pain. "We were going to talk to them about it again after tax season since it's such a busy time. Maybe a part of me wanted to believe that they were right. I told myself, maybe Madison *did* meet a guy and she'll be back. Or maybe she just had a fight with them and isn't really missing but is staying with her friends and not staying in touch. It wasn't until we talked to Franny that we realized how dire the situation had gotten and that she was the one who'd filed the police report."

Just as I'm about to ask a follow-up question, I hear someone's footsteps down the hallway on the carpet. She clears her throat.

Unlike her grandparents, who seem to put on a good show, Franny is hiding nothing.

Her eyes are bloodshot, her hair is stringy, and her skin seems to be lacking all color. She's dressed in gray sweats that make her look even more sickly and when she forces a smile on her face, she looks like she's in actual pain.

"Thanks for coming, Detective Pierce," Franny says, pulling at the bottom of her shirt and tucking her thumb underneath the fabric in a nervous fashion.

"I wanted to see how you were."

"Fine, I guess." She shrugs. "Been better."

"I was just talking to your grandparents about your sister."

"Yeah. She doesn't even know that this has happened," she says, shaking her head, tears welling up in her eyes.

"Do you think that her disappearance could have anything to do with your parents' murder?"

"I don't know," she says.

She walks over to the bar, pours herself a cup of water from the sink, and sits down on the couch in between her grandparents. The couch is so wide it looks like it could swallow her whole. She seems so small, she could disappear into the cushions without much effort.

We talk a little bit more about what happened, what she found, but nothing comes up besides what I learned from her yesterday. We make a little bit of small talk about this and that as I try to get to know them better as people. You never know what kind of things come up that would be of significance.

After a little while, I see the fatigue set in. This is not an official interview, of course, and we'll likely bring them in next week after they have a little bit of time to settle.

The forensics are currently being processed, autopsies are being performed, but that all takes time. There's no immediate evidence. There were no cameras set up. And the crime scene team is still going through the electronics they found at the house.

I fill them in on some of the details, but the information seems to tire them out even more. I don't tell them about the missing teeth. It's too gruesome and not an image that you can easily get out of your mind. Besides, I don't have any additional information. I still have no idea whether they were pulled before or after death.

"We're going to be looking into all of the clients that your parents had," I say a little while later. "We have access to their business records and their office, but there's a lot of information. Is there anyone that any of you know who was particularly antagonistic toward your parents for any reason whatsoever? Neighbors, friends, clients? There's no wrong answer here. We're just looking for leads."

The three of them look at each other, shaking their heads.

"No, we don't know of anyone. Mom and Dad never mentioned anything like that. I mean, they were working all around the clock. They had a lot of clients and they had an audit going on, but why would anyone want to kill their accountants? For what?"

"That's what we're trying to find out," I say.

"What about my sister?" Franny asks. "Are you going to look for her?"

"Of course. I'm going to file the missing person's report and we're going to have a meeting with the local news. We're going to ask for leads from anyone who knows anything about your parents' murder or your sister's case."

She nods, looking mildly pleased.

"I wish I could offer you more help, but at this point, we're just going to follow-up and do a lot of interviews with neighbors, clients, business associates. I have to warn you that this is a long process. It takes a while to get people to open up and unless someone has seen something, it's going to be a long shot."

What I don't tell any of them is that cases that aren't solved in the first forty-eight hours, with witnesses, video footage, or anything like that, take a very, very long time.

It's the obvious suspects who surface first, but the person or people who did this are either experienced or determined or both. They did their research and that makes these cases harder to solve.

Still, I hope that one of the neighbors or someone saw something. I hope that a clue comes forward. Maybe then we can get some answers.

"Can I come see you tomorrow?" Pamela asks. "At the station? See the flyer for my granddaughter, check on the case."

"Normally I would say yes, but I'm actually off this weekend," I say. "There are other people working on this case besides me, but I have a trip planned."

"You're going away?"

"I'm sorry, but we have lots of other officers who will be looking into this. As I told you, the case is currently being processed."

"What about talking to all the neighbors?" Pamela says. "You said you were going to do that."

"We are. My partner, Will, is going to do that today and over this weekend, but I just can't cancel this trip."

"Whatever." She walks me to the door and just as I turn around to apologize again, she slams it in my face.

Of course, this is my case and I know that I should probably stay home to take care of it, but the reunion isn't going to happen again and I already requested the time off.

Will can confidently carry out the interviews with the neighbors and whatever leads we get from their emails. Perhaps it's better if I come back on Saturday, instead of staying the full weekend. It's only a two and a half hour drive, after all.

13

CHARLOTTE

I get in the car with a heavy heart. I shouldn't be leaving so abruptly. This case needs me. I know that as much as anyone else. I also know that a big part of me doesn't really want to go back to Long Beach and confront what should have been discussed all of those years ago.

However, I had promised Clara that I would be there. Maybe I can go to the reunion tonight and drive back tomorrow, conduct the rest of the interviews as necessary, confirm with Will about any possible leads, and work on this case until we find the killer.

I arrive in Long Beach on a familiarly gloomy day. It's not unusual for it to be overcast since it's less than two miles from the ocean, the marine layer is thick around here. The fog only starts to dissipate sometime in the afternoon. Today, we're not so lucky.

I arrive around three and the sun is just starting to peek over the horizon. I thought that coming here would put a feeling of dread in me. But it's actually the opposite.

I'm excited. I haven't been here in years and it's surprising how much of the city has changed. There are new condos going up all over the place especially near downtown. Yet the Art Deco style of old Long Beach remains, giving it an authentic craftsman, turn-of-the-twentieth-century feel that I'm familiar with.

Driving down 2nd Avenue, I enjoy the window displays of vintage stores, the beautiful display of the fancy wine and cheese shop, and the bright neon lights of the hip, upscale boutiques. The Belmont Athletic Club, note that they do not call themselves a gym, is the place where I used the elliptical machine and took numerous Pilates classes because it was a place to hang out with my friends.

Dad thought of working out only as a means to an end. You stay fit to be healthy, but there are all the other positives of spending time with friends. That was beyond him. He was always kind of a loner in that respect. That's why I've always found it surprising that he thrived and actually enjoyed working for the FBI.

We lived by California State University Long Beach for a few years before he met my stepmother and I got a whole new family. My mother had left many years before, never to be heard from again, and it was just my dad and me living this solitary existence.

I remember distinctly that things were a lot better when I was little. But when I turned eleven or so, things changed. It's like he didn't know how to be my father anymore.

He was a stranger in a strange land. He had no idea about the music I listened to, the books I read, or the movies I was obsessed with. He didn't really care about who my friends were or the teachers who inspired me.

The few times that he saw me watching some TV drama about teenagers, he made fun of the actors and the story and I quickly learned to turn it to the news whenever he came into the room. To watch the news meant that I was interested in something interesting. No one knew at that time that the 24-hour cable news networks were nothing but banal entertainment just like everything else.

I took everything in stride back then, figured that Dad knew what was best. But in reality, it ended up being a very lonely time for me.

The sun starts to peek in through the clouds and burn away the marine layer. This was always my favorite time, out here by the ocean, when the wetness in the air dissipates just a little and warm sun finally wraps its rays around you.

My GPS takes me down Orchard Street but I go rogue. I know every street here. Quincy and Division was where I tried my first cigarette. In the alley behind Argonne and 1st, was where I had my first kiss.

I arrive on time and find street parking, in between a new Prius and an old Chevrolet. Clara lives in a two-story old Spanish style house with two huge bay windows, our dream place to live when we were young. I head up the steep staircase and drop the antique metal knocker onto her thick wooden door. When she opens the door, her eyes get big, her mouth drops open slightly, and she pulls me in close to her.

"You're here," she whispers in my ear. I feel her hot breath through my hair, and yet a shiver runs down my spine. She looks almost exactly the same as I remember her. Older, of course, but like she had grown into her face.

Clara has dark, thick hair, pale, milky white skin, and big pink lips lined generously with gloss. Her features are angular, but softer than they were when she was a kid. I know that she has fluctuated in weight a lot, going from very skinny to quite big, eventually settling, I guess, at this weight after her hysterectomy.

She holds my hand for a few moments too long, intertwining her pink manicured nails with my stubby ones. Dressed in jeans, a lightweight blouse, and an apron with lemons on it, she announces my arrival like I'm some sort of VIP guest.

"Hey, everyone. Remember Charlotte Pierce?"

Stephanie Coa is the first to stand up. Tall and elegant, she's dressed head to toe in expensive clothing, adorned with perfume. Her hair is slicked, jet black with none of the frizz it had in middle school. She came here as a child from China with her mother who expected her to study from morning to night and would never accept anything less than an A.

"You remember Steph, and Briana, of course?" Clara says.

Briana Sacks comes forward and gives me a warm hug. They both do. We all stand looking at one another, almost in awe. Briana's curvy with a big bosom that she started getting at the beginning of sixth grade.

She has beautiful olive-toned skin, and the blonde hair from a few years ago that I've seen on Facebook is gone, replaced by a dark, shiny almost jet black hue. She's wearing tight jeans, accentuating her thick behind, no longer hiding her curves like she used to when she was little and instead leaning into her Iranian body type.

There are three other girls and two guys here, some I don't remember well, but others I do. They chat and have drinks, but I stay close to Clara, Briana, and Stephanie.

"I'm making cocktails. What would you like?" Clara asks.

"Wine is good."

She has glasses of white wine pre-poured, and I opt for that just to make it easier. I look around her place, and it's beautiful. Colorful linens, a mid-century modern couch, bright without being overpowering.

There's a lot of personality in here, and Clara has always been someone who was really into the '70s as a decade. It was popular back then. There was even a show called *That '70s Show*. But Clara took it to a whole other level. She wore bell bottoms, bright orange and fuchsia colors, and even blue eyeshadow to complete the look.

I walk over to the console table and look at the pictures of her kids. "Are they here?" I ask.

She shakes her head. "No, my mom is on a trip and my husband took them to Disneyland overnight to give us the place.”

“Does your mom live with you?”

She nods.

“That must be nice.”

"Yeah, it has its positives and negatives. You know how it is.” Clara laughs, and then she remembers that no, in fact, I don't. I’ve never had my mom in my life, but I can imagine what it might be like to live with my father and the idea is not exactly appealing.

A few more guests show up and I'm left alone with Stephanie for a moment, looking at pictures of Clara’s family.

"Do you have any kids?" I ask her.

She shakes her head no. "I don't even have a boyfriend."

"Neither do I.” I smile. "But we're still young, right? Early thirties and all."

"Is thirty-three early thirties or is it bordering on mid-thirties at this point?" she asks, jokingly.

I shrug.

"I can't really say."

She drinks a few sips of her gimlet and I note that Clara has really gotten good at making cocktails.

"I wish I'd gotten one," I add. "You can get white wine anywhere, right? This is a one-time thing."

She smiles. She's dressed in long flared designer jeans which accentuate her slim, tall frame. She's a couple inches taller than I am, and wearing boots, as well, but she's so slim that you can see her collarbones and she looks almost like models do. She's so put-together, she looks like she could have walked out from a magazine ad campaign.

"So what is it that you do?" I ask her, being vaguely familiar with the fact that she is involved in tech.

"I work for startups," Stephanie says, twisting the gold ring on her index finger around in a circle. It has a delicate design and looks like it cost a couple months of my salary.

"I used to do a lot of code," she adds. "But then I moved up, got involved with a few founders, and went higher up on the food chain, so to speak. One of the companies that I have a number of shares in sold for a bunch of money and now I'm kind of in between things."

"You don't want to do that anymore?" I ask.

"Yeah, it's interesting enough, taking a company from inception to full-fledged idea with investors and then selling it to the public. But it's a big job, lots of hours, and I've got a lot of money now. Not to be crass. I can live off investments for the rest of my life and be perfectly happy."

"Wow, that's really great," I say. "I'm happy for you."

Stephanie smiles. She's not bragging, she's just sharing in the way that I've noticed sometimes wealthy people do, without taking note of the audience that they're talking to.

After chatting with Stephanie for a little while, she drifts away and I turn my attention to Briana, who leans against the wall, drinking a beer.

"So what have you been up to?" I ask.

"Nothing much. Motherhood. You know how that is."

"Yeah. How many kids do you have?"

"Three." She smiles. "It's great, but it's kind of hard being a single mom."

"Yes, it must be so hard. I'm so sorry," I say.

"Don't be, my ex-husbands were all dogs and weren't exactly supportive."

"How many exes do you have?"

"Two. Had the first two with this one tool from Colorado, and my third one, I met this guy in Florida who I thought was my perfect match. He was so supportive. He loved my kids. He said he'd be there no matter what. Then we had a baby with special needs and well, he was nowhere to be found."

"Wow, that sucks."

"Yeah. Living with my mom now too, which has its challenges as you can imagine, but I'm grateful for the babysitting and all the help that she provides."

I remember her mom worked night shift as a nurse at the children's hospital. I hardly ever saw her when we all came over to her house because, well, she was, frankly, never there.

"I heard you're a police officer?" Briana asks.

Clara and Stephanie drift over and I tell them the story all at once.

"I went to college, but then got a job at the LAPD, was there for a number of years before transferring over to Mesquite County Sheriff's Department."

I gloss over all the uncomfortable details.

"Wow. That's amazing, and you're a detective?"

"Yes." I shake my head. "Working on a big case, we have a double murder now that we're investigating, I was planning on staying the whole weekend, but I have a bunch of interviews to conduct so I'm not sure that'll be possible. I wanted to come by and visit with you all. It has been ages."

"For sure, it has."

They ask me more about my work and I fill them in about all the juicy details that people love to hear; carrying a concealed weapon, talking somebody off the ledge, solving a murder, all the exciting bits.

What I don't mention is that the job is 95% paperwork and a little bit boring and about 5% full of excitement. That's plenty.

"It's not the adrenaline rush of TV police work, but it keeps me busy," I say, summing it all up.

I stay for a number of drinks, hors d'oeuvres, and arugula salad with salmon bites. We catch up on our lives and complain about some old teachers like Mr. Holt, our 7th grade English teacher who lived with his father and never gave anyone above a B.

We talk about anything and everything except what happened that one night.

14

CHARLOTTE

Eventually everyone starts to filter out, but Briana, Clara, and Stephanie stay. Clara's busy at the bar making more cocktails. She says that daiquiris and gimlets are her specialty, but she also makes pretty good cosmopolitans and Long Island iced teas.

"It's been kind of a hobby of mine. Some people pick up cooking, I picked up making alcoholic drinks," she says without a tinge of irony. Stephanie and I take the cosmos, and are pleasantly surprised by how balanced the flavors are.

"You're definitely talented," I agree.

I offer to help Clara clean up, but she protests by waving her hand. She wants us to have more time to catch up. As we talk, I find out that Stephanie has picked up painting.

She shows us some of her pictures on her phone and I expect to ooh and aah at some basic stick drawing. What I don't expect is to find something that resembles the Dutch masters works hanging in museums.

"This is stunning," I say. "I mean, the use of color, even though it's such a dark painting. You're beyond talented, Stephanie, you have to pursue this."

"Thank you. I've now taken a couple of different painting classes, and I'm really loving it. It gets me out of my head, and well, it's something that my mom would never approve of, and, thankfully, now I don't need her approval."

It dawns on me just how hard life was for her growing up. Her single mom didn't speak English well, but was very strict about friends, parties, sleepovers, and any contact outside of school whatsoever.

"You know how I never did any sports?" Stephanie says.

I take a sip and nod.

"Well, I've always wanted to. I love being active. I love hiking. I love doing yoga. I even love going to the gym.

But as a kid, my mom had this theory that you either spend your time doing sports or you spend your time studying, and you were worse for it, if you wasted your efforts and energy on something like sports."

"I remember how much I wanted you to join the cross country team," I say. "You said you would but then you changed your mind."

Clara and Briana exchange looks. They were never sporty in any sense.

"Yeah, well, I was trying to cover up for her. It's so stupid. And I feel so dumb, but at that age I just couldn't come forward and tell you guys what my home life was really like."

"I'm glad you can tell me now," I admit.

Stephanie smiles.

"I've had way too much therapy. Plus I'm secure in where I am financially, personally, and emotionally. It's like, this is who I am, take it or leave it."

"I like that," I say. "I can sense that confidence in you."

"Well, it helps that you're absolutely gorgeous," Briana says, holding onto her own belly a little too tightly, probably feeling self-conscious. "I mean, your clothes, your heels, I just can't believe you're the same girl from before."

"I was quite nerdy," she says. "Remember those coke bottle thick glasses with the black rims?"

"Yeah." I laugh.

"Everybody wears those glasses now, but back then you were *four eyes* and just a nerd, an idiot. The truth was that I wasn't ever really that smart or that great in school, but I studied a lot, mostly because there was nothing else to do. And it kind of saved me from spending all that time with my mom."

"And what about now?" I ask. "What's your relationship like?"

"Nonexistent. Haven't talked to her in over seven years, I think," she says, trying to count in her head.

My mouth nearly drops open.

"Yeah, if you can believe it."

"Did you have a falling out?"

"The first job I had after grad school was at Google, and she thought that I should hold onto that job for dear life, that no one else would have me, and I was lucky to have it. I knew that I was worth more. I knew about the startup world. I wanted to take a chance on this company and go work for them, even though the money wasn't as good, but it was well worth it. I didn't make as much initially, but after a couple years, it got sold, and I got a really big amount of shares."

"That's so great."

"When I told her, she started telling me that it was her idea all along, instead of congratulating me. She said that she knew that I had to do that, completely gaslit me about what had really happened, and pretended that she was on my side, that we were friends. It was terrible. But at that point I'd just had enough. We only talked once every two weeks or so. And it was kind of like a rundown of her ailments, and all of these complaints she had with her so-called friends, in the community, and my achievements. I could never come to her with anything negative, or any real advice, because it would be my fault."

I rub the outside of my glass with my thumb, wanting to give her a hug.

"And so after that day," Stephanie continues. "I decided to just move on. I told her that I didn't want to hear any of that anymore and that I wanted her to apologize. I don't think I've ever heard her say, 'I'm sorry,' for anything in my whole entire life."

"What happened?" Clara asks.

"Nothing. She refused, acted like I had made it all up. So, I told her that I wouldn't speak to her again unless we could have an honest conversation. I stopped returning her calls, and two weeks later she stopped calling. She just can't be wrong. She can't bring herself to apologize, to be real, even for a second."

She looks around and sees all of us staring at her.

"God, Clara, what is in these drinks? You've totally got me buzzed. Sorry, guys. I didn't mean to dump all of this crap on you."

"No, it's good to hear something true," I say. "I mean, it was pleasant to catch up with everyone about general updates, but this is the kind of stuff I want to hear, something real."

15

CHARLOTTE

I don't know if the other girls felt nervous about coming here the way that I did, but after a few hours, everyone seems more relaxed. Girls is probably not the appropriate word for what we are, women in their thirties, but I use it as a term of endearment.

"So, where are your husband and kids?" Briana asks, looking at her watch. It's just after ten. "I thought they'd be home by now since we're staying so late."

"Yeah, I'm sorry. We should probably go," I start to say.

But Clara jumps to stop us from heading toward the door. As she moves she slams her foot into the side of the couch, sending her wincing to the floor. After checking to see if she's okay, we all crack up laughing, remembering how clumsy she was as a kid.

With a bag of frozen peas and her left foot elevated in the recliner, we all gather around as Clara tells us all of the various medical procedures she has been through as a result of her awkward movements.

"Well, I broke, I think, three or four of my toes, which they don't really do much for. I twisted innumerable number of ankles, broke one, which was one heck of a summer with a four-year-old, let me tell you. I broke two arms, twisted my wrist, and got carpal tunnel so bad I needed surgery. That wasn't really my fault though, I sat too long in a wrong position in a crappy office chair that my boss refused to upgrade. And that doesn't count all the other procedures I had."

"Like what?" I ask.

"I had endometriosis for years. It was debilitating, awful, as bad as you hear about it, and I had a few surgeries dealing with that. One made it worse, one made it better. Kind of got me back to status quo. Eventually, I had my uterus removed with a hysterectomy. And though I no longer have the pain, now I have all sorts of the hormone replacement issues that are no fun."

"Huh. Way to make us all jealous," Stephanie says in that slightly mocking tone that makes us laugh out loud.

"How about another round of drinks?" Clara offers and starts to hop out of the recliner when Briana stops her.

"My turn."

"You don't know how to make them. They have to be all measured and precise. It's a science more than an art," Clara says.

"Okay, well, how about you just tell me what you want and how to make the drink and I'll follow the directions?"

"Pour one and a half ounces of Amaretto liqueur, one ounce of simple syrup, and three-fourths of an ounce of fresh lemon juice into a cocktail shaker with ice. Shake and strain it into a glass filled with ice. Garnish with an orange slice and a maraschino cherry."

"Your ingredients are top notch. Seriously," she says approvingly, taking a few generous gulps and finishing the drink faster than all of us.

"You got to take it easy or I'm going to have to drive you home tonight," I say.

"Don't worry. After years of living in the Bay Area and having all those cocktail hours, three martini lunches, and everything else that goes along with it, I have developed quite a tolerance. It's something I'm quite proud of, if you can imagine," she says, shaking her head almost in disapproval.

"Honestly, it's pathetic. I would say almost everyone is bordering on alcoholism up there, but what can you do? It's a dog eat dog world, right?"

"And that's why I am particularly grateful for what I do for a living," Clara says. "It's not flashy. It doesn't make that much money. But, I don't have your negative perspective on life."

Clara works for a temp agency, finding employees for large scale companies. Stephanie tilts her head and gives her a warm smile.

"It must be nice to help people find work. That's something you can really be proud of," Stephanie says, with a tinge of jealousy.

"WE RECENTLY GOT a whole bunch of people in jobs at the docks. The pay is good. It's a union job, and God knows there aren't many of those left. The big project now is a new distribution center in town. My boss has been hounding me, but I can only hire people who apply. And if I don't have that many applications, what can I really do?"

"Do you find that a lot of people apply?" I ask.

"They do. But, the thing is that staffing companies are kind of an old school thing, remember from the '90s? They were pretty common in a lot of corporate environments and then they sort of dissipated. The employers know about them, and so they rely on us to find a number of people fast. But, employees often don't have any clue that we even exist. They apply to work directly through *Indeed*, *Monster*, all the usual sites. But, it's not the same having someone submit an application on your behalf. We're kind of like head hunters, but for lower pay employees. Plus, I can give them advice about their resume, how to improve it, how to word things so that it benefits them. You'd be surprised how terrible some people's resumes are. Even if they're experienced and have college degrees, they just don't tailor each one and each cover letter to the position. They apply blankly to a bunch of different places, and that's a big no-no."

"But it's time consuming to do that, right?" Briana asks. "I mean, if you're applying to like fifty jobs, you have to tailor each one?"

"Yeah, unfortunately you do. That's the expectation now from corporate. They want to know that you have read the job listing. They want to know how you fit in given your skills for that particular position. But mostly it's because the first sorting is done through a computer. Basically, a computer matches you."

"What do you mean?" I ask.

"They have a software that matches your resume and all the keywords that are found in it, and the cover letter, with the job posting. Whoever is the biggest match, whoever mentions what's mentioned in the listing as an attribute that they have, those candidates appear at the top of the pile. People who don't do that, who don't tailor their applications to the listings kind of end up screwed."

The four of us stare into space for a few moments before Briana breaks the silence by bringing up Clara's family again.

16

CHARLOTTE

"My husband's parents don't live too far from here in Huntington Beach," Clara explains. "They're all there for the evening. My mom's on a cruise for the weekend with her bridge club, so we have the place to ourselves."

I look around her three-bedroom once again. The living room is large and spacious, but the whole place is probably under two thousand square feet. Seems kind of tight for three kids, two parents, and a grandparent.

"I remember you always wanted to live here," Clara says, almost reading my mind. "In a townhouse, just like this one, upper level, bay window looking out onto the street below."

"Yeah. It just looks like such a dream, being able to walk everywhere."

"It is," Clara says. "I walk my kids to school, not too far away, couple of blocks, get groceries. Of course, Trader Joe's and the big box stores are further out, but Belmont Shore has plenty of little boutiques and stuff like that."

"Places you can't really afford to shop in," I want to say, but I don't want to be cruel.

"I know it seems like we barely fit in here," Clara says. "But it's really the best thing. Jack works in IT, but at the docks. It's a very high-security kind of place, but he works the night shift, if you can believe that. The pay is good, but obviously, the hours suck. It's on for twelve hours, off for twelve hours, that kind of thing."

"So, he works every night?" Briana asks.

"Sunday through Wednesday. He's off Thursday, Friday, Saturday. But he starts the shift at 4:00 a.m. so that he's back at 4:00 p.m., then we have dinner. We're kind of used to it now, but it was hard for a while. And instead of having Mom live somewhere else, we just have her live here. She does a lot of the cooking and cleaning, picking up the kids from school when necessary. She's just a big help."

"That's great," I say.

"But Jack's parents, they keep talking to us about moving to Huntington Beach. We'd have more space. It's more affordable. We can have a bigger place. I mean, we pay twenty-five hundred dollars for this place."

"Wow."

"And it's a three-bedroom. So it's actually kind of a good deal, but, you know, it would be good to own something one day."

We all nod, but she shakes her hands and head and shrugs our concerns off.

"Look, I don't want you to worry. We're doing very well. Yeah, we don't have a house of our own, but look, we're living right by the beach. It's great. You have to make some compromises. You either pay more money or you live in a smaller space. That's just the way it is."

"Of course."

"And we don't have the one-hundred-twenty degree heat that you do."

I smile.

"Believe it or not, you get used to it after a while."

"Yeah, that's what people always say about the cold, too, but I don't think so."

Briana finally finishes all of our drinks, second round, and Clara promptly fires her as a bartender.

"We had to wait ages. There's no way this could be your new job in case you were looking for something."

"Well, I'm not, but yeah. Sorry about that. I'm not great at following directions."

"It's not bad, this is actually delicious." Clara takes a sip and gives her an approving nod. "It's just that it took forever to make them."

"Okay, well, you can take it out of my tip," Stephanie jokes. "Oh, wait, you weren't going to leave me one."

We crack up laughing. The banter is even better, definitely much smarter than it was before. The four of us fall into a natural groove of how we were as kids. There's slight teasing, no real competition, just joking around in a good-natured kind of way.

Everyone makes fun of me for being a detective, pretending to give me reverence, but really they just give me a lot of disrespect.

When they ask me where I live, I tell them about my three-bedroom house in suburban Palm Valley.

"*You…* in a *cookie-cutter* suburb?" Briana smiles, shaking her head. "And you don't even have kids. What's your excuse?"

"I know, it's awful, isn't it?" I smile. "I mean, the two-car garage, the place for my bike, seventy-degree weather all winter, lots of hiking and mountain biking trails, and being able to swim probably ten months a year in my eighty-degree water pool. Yeah, I sold out. I sold out big time."

"So you really like it there?" Clara asks.

"I do. Summers can be kind of tough, but I get up so early that there's like four hours that I have when it's relatively cool."

"Why do you get up so early?" Stephanie asks.

"Well, I used to do it when I was a deputy, and it just makes sense especially in the summertime. It's usually in the seventies and eighties up until about nine o'clock. So if I'm up at five, I have a good amount of time to really take advantage of cool. I don't start work now until eight. So that's when I go on a hike, or a walk. All that stuff. The swimming I reserve for one hundred ten-degree days though." I smile.

"I can't believe you have your own pool. My kids would die for that."

"Mine, too," Briana agrees.

"Well, you're welcome to come over anytime."

"Sure." They give me dismissive nods.

"No, I'm serious. I mean, I use it, but not that much. I'd love for you guys to come, swim, have a long weekend. It's a three-bedroom, and the rooms are big, and there's a living room as well."

They exchange a significant glance, and I can tell that they're actually taking this under consideration. Maybe in another life, in another time, I wouldn't have made such an offer, but I feel good about it.

Sometimes you say things just to be nice, but hope that people actually don't take you up on it. In this case, I do.

The more I think about it, the more excited I get about them actually visiting. I don't know many people who know me from when I was little and for years I ran away from the few people who did.

But tonight it feels like I'm actually running *toward* something, something good.

We chat a little bit about Clara's husband, Briana's lack of husband, before settling upon the fact that Stephanie and I are both woefully single.

"So why is that?" Clara asks, looking at us in almost an accusatory way.

I shake my head, and so does Stephanie, and we giggle like school girls. "I notice you didn't ask Briana that."

"Hey, I've been married too many times," Briana points out. "I'm done with men, okay. The last one said he was going to stick around. He was going to be a good egg. He was going to be there for our kids, but no. So I'm done."

"Done as in no more dating, or done as in switching over to women?" I smile.

She shakes her head. "Well, hey, that's actually not a terrible idea."

And we all laugh.

"Quit trying to avoid the question," Clara says, turning her attention to me and Stephanie. "You two have seriously have never been married before? You're thirty-three years old."

"Thirty-four," Stephanie says.

"I know, pathetic," I add.

"Hey." Briana raises her hand, pushing her dark black hair out of her face. "I know, I read about this online. Are you one of those people who are just happy to be single? You're celebrating yourself and going to marry yourself or something like that?"

"Well, I can't speak for Stephanie, but that's a no for me," I say. "I'm definitely not going to marry myself."

"You know what I mean. Like you just like being solo, and that's just how it is?" Then she leans over and whispers, "You know you can tell us if you're gay, right? We're totally okay with it."

"I'm not, but thank you anyway. And ditto to all of you," I say, pointing at each one demonstratively.

"Well, I can't speak for Charlotte, but I dated a few guys. It didn't work out and that's pretty much it."

"Anyone serious?" I ask.

"Actually, no, maybe two, three months, but that's it."

"Never lived with anyone?" I ask.

She shakes her head. "So as far as being solo, and being happy about it, I think I fit into that category. It's just hard for me to imagine living with a guy or even a roommate at this point. I mean, a relationship, maybe, but it seems like all the good ones are taken, or they come with ex-wives and kids, and no offense to you all with kids, but I don't know if I want them."

"You don't want kids?" Clara asks. "Are you serious?"

Stephanie nods her head.

"Okay. Well, you have to meet my kids. And then I think you'll want them."

We all burst out laughing.

"I'm happy to meet them but don't get upset if I don't want any kids after. I just don't think I was born with that maternal instinct. Besides, my mom really messed me up."

"And what about you?" They turn their attention to me.

"What's your situation?"

17

CHARLOTTE

"What about you, Charlotte?" Stephanie changes the conversation after sharing more than enough. "How come *you* aren't married with children?" she says, her tone of voice drenched in sarcasm.

I shrug. "Just doesn't work out for some people."

"But you can't give up. I mean, *if* that's what you want," Briana says.

"Honestly, as far as kids are concerned, I really don't know. I've never had a strong mothering instinct, but I can imagine that it's something that I would enjoy, but a relationship? I don't know."

"What are you talking about? You've given up on men, too?" Clara asks.

"No, I wouldn't say that. It's just that things are kind of rough with my ex."

"Do tell."

They all move a few inches closer.

It's interesting talking to people who you haven't spoken to for years and don't know your story inside and out. I have a couple of friends back in Palm Valley, but they've known my ex personally, and it's kind of hard to talk to them about him since they do have that inside knowledge.

"We were together for three years," I say. "We transferred out of the LAPD at the same time. We were planning on getting married, engaged, having a wedding. And we bought this house that we just happened to see. We weren't in the market, but it was a great deal. And then one day, he started ghosting me. Not answering text messages, saying that he was busy, that kind of thing. I tried to talk to him about it, but he was still being a little shady. So, I followed him once after work."

"And?" Clara asks.

"He was having an affair with a crime scene investigator. It was her first year there. From what I heard, I never talked to her directly, but she swore that she had no idea that we were a couple. We kept things private. Not that many people in the department knew. Anyway, the house ended up being in my name because I had good credit. He had this good job, but he spent too much money on toys: motorcycle, ATV, all that stuff that cluttered up the garage. When I talked to him about it, our lease was up at our apartment and it was time to move. He said that he didn't think we were a good fit. That's why he started seeing that other girl. She was easier, simpler. Plus her dad wasn't in the FBI, constantly making him feel inferior about his career."

"What do you mean?" Briana asks, and I fill her in on my dad's attitude toward my current job. "Did he have that same opinion about your ex-fiancé? What's his name?"

"Dale Herbert. He only applied and my dad went out of his way to block his application."

"Really?"

"Yeah. He just didn't think he had the *'moral fiber'* required for that job, and that was before he found out that he had cheated on me. And of course after our relationship fell apart, Dad essentially confirmed his opinions, but I have a feeling that he did it solely for the purpose of... I don't know, messing with us? Messing with me? He never thought that Dale and I were a good fit, he didn't like him, and he wasn't shy about expressing his feelings."

"God, that sucks," Briana says. "Does your ex still work with you?"

"Yeah. We had just declared our relationship to human resources so after we broke up, had to do that once again. That was a great afternoon," I say sarcastically. "But it had to be done and luckily, HR is now pretty careful about not assigning us the same case."

"And what happened with Dale and that girl?" Stephanie asks.

"They dated for about a year and then she cheated on him. So that was, I guess, some consolation. What goes around comes around."

They laugh, and I do, too. At first, it's a bit uncomfortable, but then I just let myself go and really find the humor in the absurdity.

"Are you okay, Charlotte?" Stephanie puts her hand on mine.

"Yeah, I'm fine," I say. "It's just so stupid. I'm still talking about this, what, two years later? Still living in that house."

"You didn't want to sell it?"

"I like it. It's a nice house. We got a really good deal and it's probably appreciated seventy thousand dollars since then. So, I don't see a reason to give it up. At least I decorated it myself how I wanted it, avoiding everything that he'd picked out."

"That's something. Besides, he never moved in, right?"

"Yeah," I say.

There's a long pause where no one says anything and I feel like I really brought the evening down.

I told myself that if I were to talk about Dale, it would be an upbeat, nice kind of way, and I wouldn't come off so bitter. But the thing is that I am angry.

He wasted my time and then he didn't have the decency to tell me that he didn't want to be with me anymore, and instead just moved on, tried to see if things would be better with Alicia before jumping ship. It's a coward's way out, and only cowards do that.

Unfortunately, there are way too many of them out there.

I look at my old friends and I wonder, how many of them have been cheated on and how many of them have done the cheating?

I don't have to wonder for long as they all come forward and share their stories of disappointing husbands and exes.

Unfortunately, or perhaps fortunately, I'm not alone in my misgivings about getting into more relationships especially with people who just don't give a damn.

"Listen, we've all been through a lot. We've all been with our share of crappy men. Let's just raise our glasses of Amaretto sours," Clara says, putting hers high above her head. "Let's just celebrate that we were able to reconnect after all of this time and still be friends."

"Here, here," we all say, clinking.

"Because the truth is when I decided to put this event together, I wasn't sure how it was going to turn out," Clara adds, and we laugh.

"Yeah, me either," Stephanie agrees. "I honestly thought that I was going to hate you all. I mean, I was curious to come and see what you were up to, but never thought that we would actually connect."

"Me either," I agree. We drink up, looking deep into each other's eyes.

That's when I remember the secret that we had all shared and buried all of those years ago. If I were to bring this up now, the whole night would be ruined. Besides, we're too drunk to talk about it in any meaningful way.

But if we don't talk about it now, when?

When would be a good time, if ever?

We clink our glasses again and finish the last of our drinks. No one's having anymore if we want to make it to our hotel rooms in one piece.

"What do you guys think about staying over?" Clara asks. "I have room. My kids, husband, and Mom are gone. I have plenty of sleeping bags and blow up mattresses."

"My stuff's in the car," Briana points out.

"Yeah. Mine, too." Stephanie nods.

"I wouldn't want to drive drunk," I say. "As long as it's not an imposition."

"No, not at all."

18

CHARLOTTE

Clara gets all of our sleeping stuff out. She wasn't kidding when she said that she had plenty. It seems like one of the back closets is entirely devoted to sleepover materials. There are blow-up mattresses, sleeping bags, extra towels, anything and everything you could think of.

She quickly blows up three twin mattresses and covers them up with linens. We agree to all stay in the living room, even though she offers her kids' and mom's bedrooms.

"There's no need for that," Stephanie says. "We're all comfortable out here. If you have a fourth mattress or you want to take the couch, we'd love to have you. It could be a sleepover like we had when we were kids."

There was a time in seventh grade where we slept over at each other's houses almost all the time. Clara and Briana's places were preferred. Stephanie's was off limits. And mine was used only twice when my father was out of town. It's not that he was against sleepovers. He thought that they were frivolous and the idea of hosting one annoyed the crap out of him.

He didn't seem to mind *me* sleeping over, however, and begrudgingly agreed, but only after I did all of my homework and ran the requisite three miles. The workout ethic was more about building a habit and bettering yourself rather than staying fit. It was about having it be done, and that's why he always did his five miles every morning.

"Wow, this really does feel like old times," Briana says, lying down on the mattress after coming out of the bathroom dressed in an oversized nightie.

Stephanie wears a matching set with embroidery on the sides, clearly expensive and probably from Neiman Marcus. It fits her just so, and I actually wonder if it's tailored.

As for me, I have a loose pair of leggings and a slim fit T-shirt that's one of my favorites. Unfortunately, it's practically threadbare at this point, and I'm a little bit embarrassed about everyone seeing it.

Only Clara seems to be in her usual long-sleeve shirt and matching pajama pants, the ones that I'd seen at Target only a few days ago.

"Yeah, this totally brings back memories except for I'm not lying on the hardwood floor in a very thin sleeping bag," I say, pointing to Clara, and she bursts out laughing.

"That's right. My mom's hardwood floors! Remember the ones that she discovered after I ran through the sliding glass door."

"Yeah, you lost so much blood, you almost died. But at least she found that there were nice hardwood floors under all of that carpet. Still can't believe that they couldn't get the blood out," I add.

"They were nice," she says. "I mean, why would people cover them up?"

"Because carpet is comfortable," I say.

"You have it, don't you?" Stephanie points at me.

"Guilty as charged," I admit. "I know, it's very old-fashioned or whatever, but yes, I do have it. Yes, I like to sit on it. And yes, I replaced the old carpet in my house with new carpet, rather than tile or vinyl flooring or hardwood floors. I just like doing yoga on it without a mat. I like walking barefoot and being warm and soft. So sue me."

They all giggle, and Stephanie pretends to write me a ticket for poor taste.

Our conversation goes in comfortable loops. The alcohol is starting to wear off, but our comfort with one another isn't. The things that we needed two drinks before to admit or say out loud suddenly come out without any prompting whatsoever.

Around one in the morning, I look at them and realize that it's really now or never.

I've waited long enough, hesitated long enough.

She invited us here for a reunion, right? To rehash the past, to talk about what happened.

So, that's what I have to do.

"Hey, do you guys remember Kelsey Hall?" I ask.

We're still laughing, talking about Mrs. Williamson in sixth grade and the harsh grades she gave out in English class for even the smallest grammatical errors.

But when I bring up Kelsey's name, silence falls in the place and I hear my tongue make a slight sound leaving the roof of my mouth.

No one wants to say it. No one wants to admit to it.

But after a long, uncomfortable pause, Clara finally says, "Of course, I remember Kelsey."

KELSEY HALL WAS our fifth friend. There was initially just a clique of Clara and Briana, me and Stephanie. But Kelsey had just moved from Seattle and we were assigned to work on a project together and bonded for our mutual love of *Dawson's Creek*.

Kelsey wasn't the type of girl that everyone would want to be friends with, and so the popular kids immediately wrote her off. She had vintage clothes, the sassy attitude, and a know-it-all kind of swagger that was immediately attractive to us.

She was confident, if a little arrogant. She had dark hair, big blue eyes, and a wide face that she framed with Jackie O sunglasses. Her dark hair was cut short right above the ear in that cool hipster style that was a little too outgoing for that age.

When she pulled her hair up in a ponytail, she revealed that the bottom half of her head was shaved but at that point we were already friends and that made her even cooler. Everything about her was out of the norm and exotic. And that was even before she revealed that she had a tattoo.

Kelsey was a breath of fresh air. She was unlike anyone I have ever met before. She was outgoing and fun, sarcastic, and she seemed to have an insurmountable amount of clothing that she could style in a variety of different ways.

"Do you remember how fashionable she was?" Briana asks. "She could take any old thing and add a belt, a headband, some necklace, accessorize it every which way. And it would be brand new."

I wasn't ever really into clothes, but I remember how she blew me away with her approach. It's like she didn't need to have the most expensive or the nicest clothes. You just have to have style and know what to do and how to wear it. More memories spring up.

Stephanie laughs about how her mom was against Halloween.

"I had to come to school without a costume and Kelsey wouldn't hear of it. Instead, she got me all dolled up with just a little bit of makeup, nail polish, and accessories. She rolled up my pants, I remember, to make them short, just below the knee, put my socks up, put all of these freckles on my face, and stuck my hair out with hairspray. Suddenly, I was Scarecrow from *The Wizard of Oz*. Wasn't my first choice, but it was better than having no costume at all.

"She had a flair for that kind of thing. Didn't she?" I say. "She was so fearless. If some look didn't work out, well, it didn't matter. She would try something else. She said there were no fashion mistakes because there were no mistakes when you made art. There are just certain things that didn't work."

"That's such a good way of thinking about it," Briana agrees. "I remember I was so worried about every single thing that I wore. Did it match? Was it in style? Did it accentuate my body or make me look drab? There were all these rules and regulations in magazines about what you should and shouldn't wear. Remember, it was all about matching your skin tone to whatever season you were, fall, winter, spring, or summer, whatever the hell that means. But with Kelsey there, it was like, no, you could have fun with fashion and you could still be incredibly stylish."

"Wait, we're missing something!" Clara says, grabbing her phone and looking through her music library.

She places her phone into the speakers. When "Just a Girl" by No Doubt starts to blast, my eyes begin to water.

Kelsey had played it on her Walkman constantly. She was obsessed with it even though it had come out years before, in 1995.

We play it on loop just like we did at our sleepovers all of those years ago and miss our friend.

19

CHARLOTTE

The first bars of No Doubt's song immediately transport me back to the lunchroom in middle school. I had just plopped down my plastic tray next to Briana who introduced Kelsey and said, "She's going to eat with us."

When Kelsey waved her hand to say hi, I noticed that each of her fingers were adorned with thick silver rings. Her hair bounced when she moved. I looked at the names of bands that were doodled onto her Trapper Keeper in blue and black ink: Babes in Toyland, 7 Year Bitch, and Hole. Most were lesser known female grunge bands out of the Pacific Northwest and she educated us about what made them so cool.

Kelsey had only been there for a week or so. Since the middle school was so large with so many different classes, her presence hadn't made much of an impact.

There were cliques, of course. There were the popular kids, the guys who were good at sports and the girls who did dance, the nerds who were obsessed with *Lord of the Rings* and little groups like ours that didn't belong in one place or another.

I was on the newspaper and ran track and did swimming. Briana and Clara were on the yearbook, and Stephanie wasn't allowed to do any activities that wouldn't help her get into a really good college. And for some reason, sports were out.

Of course, whatever memories come up about Kelsey that are positive are largely balanced with what happened that fateful night that the four of us are still yet to talk about.

With the booze wearing off and the comfort level increasing, I decide to test the waters.

"Have any of you thought about what happened to Kelsey?" I ask.

The room falls silent. I'm sitting on my blow-up mattress, legs crossed, arms by my sides. Briana's lying down on her stomach. Clara's on her back and Stephanie has her legs propped up to her chest.

Everyone suddenly avoids all eye contact with everyone else. We all know what we did, but we aren't exactly excited to admit it.

"Have you?" Clara asks.

"Of course," I admit.

Everyone nods simultaneously.

"That was really messed up," Stephanie says. I scrunch up my shoulder and then relax.

"We shouldn't have lied, but every hour that passed just made it worse and I couldn't bring myself to say anything," Briana finally admits.

I give her a shrug and a reassuring smile.

"Yeah. I feel the same way. But what about all these years later? She's still missing," I say. "I check on her case every year or so, and she's gone cold case. No one knows anything."

"What about her family?" Briana asks.

"Her parents moved back to Seattle a couple of years after her disappearance. There were a few things in the paper about them having anniversary remembrances, putting together events down here to try to bring attention to her story. But as far as anyone knows, she's still missing."

"Do you think it's our fault?" Briana asks. "I mean, as a cop, do you think we're at fault?"

"What's your professional experience tell you?" Stephanie asks.

"I think that we didn't help matters. We were obviously stupid and scared and had already lied so much. After a while, admitting to the shame of what we had done just became unbearable, at least to me," I say. "I don't know about everyone else."

They nod in unison.

Briana picks at her nail polish.

Clara fidgets with a blanket.

Stephanie twirls her hair.

We're all here, but not here. We want to talk about this, but even twenty years later, it seems like it's too soon. I know I have to push them, but that means that I have to push myself.

"I've carried the secret with me for a long time," I say. "And when I saw your invitation, I figured if you wanted to talk about it, maybe do something about it, maybe that's why you invited us here?"

Clara shrugs. "Yeah. Part of me maybe, but I'm not sure. There were all those other people that I wanted to get together with as well. But yeah, I guess you could say that."

I know how she feels. The ambivalence, the disgust with your own actions. We didn't do anything to hurt her directly, but the fact that we didn't come forward and didn't tell the authorities exactly where we had been and what we had done and what we were doing there contributed greatly to her still being missing.

"We made a lot of mistakes," I say. "You know that as well as I do, but I wonder if it's time to make this right. To talk about *that night*."

"Are you going to try to look for her?"

I shrug. "Yeah, I think so. That case has haunted me. I mean, I was such an integral part of what happened and I felt responsible."

"You didn't take her."

"No, of course not. But you all know as well as I do, that if we hadn't lied about not being at that concert, they would've had a lot more leads."

"She might still be missing," Clara says.

"Of course, that's undeniably true, but we didn't even give her a chance. I was thinking that maybe we could talk about it, everything that happened, and I can match that with my own recollection.

Maybe we'd have a better idea on how to help and where to start. I can reach out to the police —"

"Would we get in trouble?" Briana cuts me off.

Her words linger and hang in the air between us all. Instead of answering with a lie, I just wait and listen like everyone else.

20

CHARLOTTE

When we were thirteen years old, a couple months before our graduation from eighth grade, we desperately wanted to go to the System of a Down concert at the Shrine Auditorium in LA. It was going to be an epic show and we didn't want to miss it.

Stephanie's mom would never say yes so she didn't even bother asking. She barely let her meet up with friends, let alone attend a concert. Briana and Clara's moms were more lenient and my dad agreed to let me go. But then the week of, he changed his mind. He was angry with something about work. I overheard him on the phone and when I got a B on a test, he took it out on me.

"No, absolutely not. You only get to go if you get straight As. Otherwise I don't want to hear about it," he said.

"I already got the tickets," I said. I paid with my own money.

"I don't care. You know the rules. You get As or else. It's a privilege to go to a concert. A privilege that you did not earn."

I gritted my teeth, argued with him some more, but he wouldn't budge. Kelsey's parents were similarly displeased and uninterested.

The concert was a big deal and we were young. No adults would be present except all of those attending and, now looking back, I wouldn't want any thirteen year olds to go either.

But the five of us developed a plan. We all said that we were sleeping over at each other's houses. I'm a little vague on exactly what we told our parents but I think Briana and I were supposedly sleeping over at Clara's.

Clara was sleeping over at Briana's. Stephanie's mom finally relented and let her go as well.

Our parents were probably relieved that the sleepover became a nice alternative to a concert full of twenty-somethings, alcohol, and drugs.

What they didn't know was that it was a lie.

There were no Ubers back then. We were underage and too young to drive. So we took the bus. It took almost two hours to get there through lots of seedy neighborhoods. But we got there. We walked the last couple of blocks to the venue, floating on cloud nine.

Clara had the idea of sneaking in some alcohol and she put some wine coolers into bottles masquerading as juice. I sipped on mine, but everyone else indulged lavishly and by the time the concert started, we were all pretty much sloshed. All I remember is screaming the words at the top of my lungs, dancing and smiling so widely that my cheeks hurt.

It was the best night of my life up until that point and it would've stayed that way if something hadn't happened.

Since we weren't technically staying at anyone's house and we'd lied about the sleepovers, we decided to pool our money together for a motel room.

The low-rise, two story building half a mile away was relatively clean and with only one pubic hair in the drain. It cost $65, which was a lot of money for us, but split five ways it was manageable. We had booked it earlier, worried that we wouldn't have a place to stay for the night and it wasn't too far away from the venue, walking distance.

After the concert, we all went to the bathroom together and that was when Kelsey realized that she'd left her scarf in her seat. It wasn't a purse so she doubted anyone would've taken it. My stomach was cramping from the alcohol and Clara was throwing up. So, Stephanie and Briana stayed with us in the bathroom while Kelsey went back to her seat by herself.

That was the last time that any of us saw her.

She disappeared.

Fifteen minutes later, Stephanie and I angrily made our way back to our seats. My stomach was in knots and I could barely walk but Clara was in terrible shape, with her head buried in the toilet bowl, so Briana stayed with her.

When we got to the seat, neither the scarf nor Kelsey were anywhere to be found.

Maybe she got lost, I thought.

She had to be here somewhere. The theater was still filled with people.

There were thousands of seats and not everyone left at the same time. Hundreds of intoxicated people were leaning on walls, trying to make sense of the night.

Once we confirmed that she wasn't there, we went back to the bathroom and told them that we had no idea where she was. Stephanie threw up while Briana and I just suffered in silence, trying to drink a lot of water to make our minds work a little better.

Minutes ticked by like hours and still, she was nowhere to be found. We looked behind most doors, walked around for hours, but still nothing.

Then there was a decision to be made.

Did we tell the security guards that she was gone so they could call the police or did we keep quiet and go to the motel room on the off chance that she would be there?

We had paid for the motel in cash a couple of days ago and she knew where it was. There was a good chance she might have gone there if she got separated and couldn't find us. This was years before smart phones or even cell phones were ubiquitous. None of our parents let us have them.

I can't remember whose idea it was but we decided to go to the motel and at least check for her.

Knowing what I know now, we should have told the security guards. We should have called 911 but at that point we were just thinking about ourselves.

We were scared thirteen year olds, after all, terrified of facing the wrath of our parents.

We weren't supposed to be there. We weren't supposed to be drunk and we just wanted to forget that we'd ever made that mistake.

Mostly, though, we couldn't imagine that anything had really happened to our friend.

21

CHARLOTTE

One of the reasons I wanted to come here was to get *their* stories.

Was there something that I missed, misremembered, didn't understand?

I know that we have wasted lots of time. We should have gone straight to the police. We were scared, stupid girls who had snuck out to a concert we weren't allowed to go to, lied about sleeping over at each other's houses, got an illicit hotel room, and got really drunk.

"Why did we ever go to that hotel room?" Clara asks. "I mean, didn't we know that there was no way she was going to be there?"

"We were just clinging on to hope," Briana says.

"For some reason, we believed that she might be there," I add. "At least that was my recollection. We wanted her to be there because then she wouldn't be missing."

"She just went to get her scarf," Stephanie says. "How did she disappear? Where did she go?"

They all looked to me. I'm the detective, the experienced party in this situation. The problem is that I'm anything but that. I'm just as guilty as they are for keeping it a secret and then never talking about it.

"I know this might not be the best time. I don't know how you all are feeling right now, but I want you to talk to me. I want you to give me your statements. I'll record them right here because I'm looking into this case."

"What do you mean?" Briana asks.

"It's nothing official. And, of course, I realize that I am as guilty as anyone else here, but the more time that passes, the more I feel like we owe her to find out the truth. Like maybe somewhere out there, she still exists. You know?"

"There's no way," Briana says. "Someone took her and killed her."

"No one ever found the body," I point out.

"So you don't think that she's dead?" Clara asks, cracking her knuckles. Her nails are long, but not exactly elegant, bitten down and picked at and then covered up with acrylic nails that seem too much like a DIY job.

They're all looking to me to give them some hope, and I'm just pulling away. I feel it within me. I was the one who brought this up, opened this wound, and now I'm struggling.

But if I want their stories, their statements, I need to get them to open up.

This is just going to be for my own investigation. It's nothing official yet. I have no jurisdiction and I'm a witness.

"I don't know whether she's dead or not," I say. "All I know is that Kelsey was our friend. And she went missing that day. And we had a responsibility to her. I know that we were drunk, that we lied to our parents, and that we would get in a lot of trouble. I know that we wanted to be these grown-ups, go to a concert, keep the party going at a motel, but…I now regret that we never told anyone. I know that you all do as well."

"I just wish that we hadn't gotten that hotel room in the first place," Clara said. "We could have just had a sleepover at my house, then we would have to tell someone about her disappearance."

"You were still not allowed to go to the concert," I say. "The problem is not regretting one part of the evening. It's the whole thing, but mainly just *not* coming forward when we needed to and when she needed us. And keeping it a secret for all of these years."

"Are we going to get in trouble?" Stephanie asks.

The confident, outgoing woman who has been sitting in front of me the whole evening is gone. Her hair is still silky straight, her makeup has just a little bit of wear and tear on the sides of her eyeliner, but before me sits a frightened thirteen-year-old girl, who probably had the most to lose that night.

I saw her mom hit her once, in the school's parking lot, with a little baton that she kept in her purse. She must have traveled with it, keeping it close by in case her daughter 'got out of line' and would need a beating.

Stephanie looks petrified, practically shaking. But this time, she's afraid of the police.

"I'm sorry," she whispers, sucking in air. "You're right. You're right about everything. Whatever might happen, to me, to us. It's nothing in comparison to what already happened to Kelsey, and she didn't deserve any of that."

"Kelsey was a little girl and we should have stood up for her," Briana says.

"Let's not dwell on what we should have done, or could have done," I say, taking charge. "This case is cold. There may be some people working on it, but there are no leads. When her parents reported her missing and called all of us, we continued to lie. Now I want to find out something that's true. Where did she say that she was staying at?"

"My house." Clara hangs her head.

WE TALK well into the night. I seem to help put their minds at ease a little bit, and I try to be that comfort space that I still can't find for myself. The voice recorder runs as we all reminisce about the past and about what happened that night.

"So what happened exactly?" I turn to Clara to get a clarification. "Kelsey told her parents that she was staying at your house, but your mom was away that night?"

Somehow the memory of all of this escaped me.

"Yeah." Clara nods. "Remember how we all told different stories to all of our parents so that we could get the hotel room together? Well, she told her dad that she was staying over. When he came to talk to me at school, I nearly lost it. It was right after the last bell and I was just about to catch my bus home and he was just there standing…distraught. He asked me what happened and I just pretended that I had no idea what he was talking about. I didn't want to meet his eyes, but I needed him to believe me."

"So what did you tell him?" I ask.

"I told him that she never came. That we had this plan, but my mom was going to be out of town and I canceled it the day before. I thought that she was just going to be at home."

I bite the inside of my lip. She doesn't know this, but this sent the detectives and everyone working on this case in a completely different direction.

If we had come forward and told the authorities that she went missing from the concert venue, they would've probably checked the exits, the videotapes, and they might have found something.

I didn't know this at that time, of course, and neither did Clara. Instead, we used one lie to cover up another.

"You have to understand," Clara says. "I just couldn't come forward because I couldn't tell them that she did sleep over because then they would talk to my mom. This way, the sleepover got changed. As far as my mom was concerned, I was still staying at Briana's and that's what she told them."

"Did they confirm that alibi?" I ask.

"I don't know. That was the last time anyone ever talked to us."

What a big misstep, I think to myself.

"What's going on, Charlotte?"

"I don't know. I'm just thinking this through from the perspective of the police."

"And what does that mean?" Briana asks.

"It's complicated. They didn't do a very good job. They should have confirmed the alibi. They should have talked to your parents and then to Briana's parents to make sure that you *actually* slept over and that you weren't lying. But I guess they didn't. I remember this case was on the news and then it kind of wasn't."

"Her parents became the primary suspects," Stephanie adds.

"They did?" Briana gasps.

I nod. "Haven't you ever looked up anything about it?"

"No." Briana shakes her head.

"Me either," Clara admits. "At least not much."

I understand their trepidation and where they're coming from.

At that time we just wanted to put it out of our minds. We didn't want to think about it. It's almost like it didn't happen.

"I remember," I start to say, "when we first got to that motel room, how much I was praying for her to be there. I thought that if I just believed and wished strong enough, then I could make it happen. I could manifest her and everything would be fine."

"Me, too. Didn't exactly work out, did it?" Clara shrugs.

"No, not at all and it was just a series of mistakes," Stephanie sighs. "I mean, who would've thought that she would be gone just like that? Poof. I remember even thinking that maybe her parents came to pick her up from the concert. Maybe she got in touch with them somehow with a payphone, who knows. But no, it was nothing like that."

"The whole thing was a disaster, but the cops didn't do a good job either," I point out. "They focused all their attention on the parents. I don't know exactly why or what their alibi was, but it was a mistake. Of course, our lies complicated everything."

"Is that why her parents moved away?" Clara asks.

I nod. "Pretty certain. Who would want to live somewhere where everyone thinks you killed your daughter?"

22

CHARLOTTE

The following morning, I review my notes. We did get a little bit of sleep. Not much at all, but everyone feels positive about what we have talked about.

Clara scrambles up eggs, puts a couple frozen waffles in the toaster, and Stephanie and I cut up strawberries and wash blueberries. Stephanie sits cross-legged on the couch, all of the pillows, blankets, and everything else have been cleaned up. Staring out of the window, she is lost in thought but when she catches me looking, she gives me a reassuring smile.

I have the recording to go through and I still have to make a lot of notes. We've all said a lot. Taken back a lot. For one, we couldn't even agree about the color of her scarf and what she was wearing that night. Briana insisted that it was a Nirvana shirt while everyone else was certain that it was from some little known band that only she and a handful of other people knew about from the Northwest.

There are so many holes to fill.

"Thanks for doing this, Charlotte," Clara says when we all sit down around her breakfast table. It's a vintage piece from the American Cancer Society Thrift Store down the street. I like the way that Clara says *vintage piece*, taking pride in the ownership, even though to me, it looks a little bit old and ratty and hardly impressive at all.

But then again, what do I know about interior design? I got all of my stuff from Wayfair and Amazon and called it a day.

Before taking a sip of my tea, I lift up my cup and say, "Thank you so much, Clara, for putting all of this together. This has been an incredible night. Not one that I will soon forget."

"You're welcome." She looks down shyly.

Everyone joins me and for a moment we forget about everything else that happened last night and just enjoy breakfast.

"And thank you to Charlotte," Briana says, "for talking about Kelsey again. I've thought about her often and I just haven't had... I don't know what to call it. The energy, the willpower, to look into it more. I haven't even read any of the newspaper articles or tried to find anything about it on YouTube. I don't even know if they ever made any *Dateline* episodes."

"They didn't," I say.

"I've looked, but I will do more research. I'm just getting started myself but I wanted to talk to you all about that night to get your recollections."

"You mentioned that the cops made some mistakes, too?" Stephanie says.

I nod.

"Yeah, they did. I mean, we shouldn't have lied. It was terrible. But if they had done just a little bit more work, they would've caught us in our lies and they could have explained to us, exactly what the repercussions of those lies were."

"What do you mean?" Clara asks.

"I deal with that a lot. That's why I kind of have sympathy for the people that we were. Teenagers come to the station, make statements to me about all sorts of improbable things. I take them at their word. Investigate. But then I press them and find that one part of it is a lie and then another, and then you tell them that they have to tell you the truth."

They all sit back a little bit.

"It's the right thing to do," I continue. "Especially if they have a friend who's missing. I'm angry that no one did that. I mean, we lied, but the cops should have pressed us a little bit more. And if they had, if they'd come to talk to your mom, they would've found out that we made up this whole thing. It probably wouldn't have taken that much prodding for us to come forward."

I'm talking out loud now, words are coming out of my mouth as quickly as they pop into my head.

"So, what are you going to do now?" Briana asks.

"I have to get back home. I have a big investigation that I'm in charge of and it's a double murder but I'm going to work on this. I'm going to listen to the recording, take notes, reach out to the police. Not right away, but as soon as I can."

"You promise to stay in touch?" Clara asks. "About any developments?"

"Of course. And if any of you think of anything else, please call me, text me, whatever."

"You think there's any chance we can find her?" Stephanie asks.

"That I don't know. Her body was never found, which is good, but it also leaves so many unanswered questions."

———

ON THE ENTIRE drive back home, I think about nothing but the reunion and the secret that we have kept. I'm coming back a whole day early hungover and badly in need of sleep because I just received a call from the lieutenant and a request to come back and handle the Dillard murders.

There are neighbors to interview, acquaintances to talk to, follow-ups to make with both Franny and the grandparents. And another missing persons case to investigate.

But the person that continues to stay on my mind is Kelsey Hall, someone I admired with my whole heart. Even if I hadn't, I owe her something.

We all did.

Finally, all of these years later, I am in the position to maybe reopen the case, at least give statements to the police about our involvement and how different the circumstances were under which she disappeared.

When I get back to Palm Valley, I head straight to the office, briefly stopping by the bathroom to check on the state of my appearance. Not great would be an understatement.

I had washed my hair the day before and it's only gotten a little bit of grease in it now, but still probably in need of some dry shampoo. I reapplied my makeup this morning, which makes me look a little bit more lively and fresh, but the hangover is alive and well, keeping its stronghold on me.

I pull my hair up in a loose bun and look at my gray jeans that are a little too tight from all the bloat. My black and white T-shirt blouse has puffy sleeves, but it's a T-shirt nevertheless, which is good for the warm eighty-two degree day. In fact, I wish I were wearing shorts, but again, that would be unprofessional.

I meet with the lieutenant, who apologizes briefly for cutting my time off short. It's Saturday morning, not too busy in the office. A time when people usually catch up on paperwork, but today the whole place is abuzz. You don't have a double murder and a missing nineteen-year-old that's possibly connected to it and not have a department as small as this one rather excited.

"We have a press conference scheduled for 11:00 a.m.," Lieutenant Soderman says, looking flustered.

He's out of breath, wearing last night's shirt with a wilted collar. His dress pants are wrinkled and I wonder if he slept on the couch in his office, something that has become a habit of his recently. It wouldn't have anything to do with the case, however.

He and his wife are going through some problems. He's been drinking for years, but it has gotten a lot worse recently. Never on the job, he's too professional for that. But his personal time is largely taken up with alcohol.

His wife, Mitzi, a no-nonsense Midwesterner with an accent to match, is someone I've only met a handful of times at some police fundraisers, the 5K run, and a few barbecues.

She has always been pleasant enough, but she's not good at being the long suffering wife of a lieutenant who works too many hours. Even in a small town like this, his job should probably have two people doing it. There's all the direct management of the deputies, detectives, and the caseloads, as well as the paperwork and the public relations with the local news, TV, and print that he has very little patience for. Let alone working with the Mesquite County higher-ups and all of the politics that he has absolutely no energy for.

Frankly, besides dealing with the media, Lieutenant Soderman is pretty well adapted to his job and its responsibilities. But a double murder and a missing persons case would put pressure on anyone.

There're others involved that help pick up the slack, but it's the initiative that's needed. And I'm worried that with his antithesis toward the media and their involvement in anything to do with crime, it's going to make this case harder to solve.

Lieutenant Soderman has a strong sweet tooth and he loves starting the day with a 72-ounce Diet Coke and a bagel. He rubs his thick hands gently across his substantial stomach, sitting back in his office chair.

"I want you to make the statement to the news people," he says.

23

CHARLOTTE

Press conferences involve an air of authority, clean clothes, a good script to read, and enough information to provide to the public to have something to go on.

I have only a couple of hours to prepare and I spend most of them working on the text. I'm going to be the face of this investigation. And as an attractive woman with sandy blonde hair, who's in her early thirties, I know that I'm a better face than say, Lieutenant Soderman.

People are going to pay attention already due to the nature of the crimes, but they may also pay attention to who I am. Optics of true crime and reality television are not lost on me. I have a nice jacket, blouse, and dress pants in my locker, just in case I have to make a public appearance.

This has happened to me once before. Lieutenant Soderman didn't want to talk to the media and I had to talk to Desert Daily News, give them quotes and be subjected to their photography. I was not dressed appropriately and later got talked to about that by the same lieutenant who didn't want to do it himself.

Since this is going to be a news conference, KTLA, Desert Daily News, and who knows what other independent reporters are going to be present. I've always enjoyed writing and I work on my script carefully.

What many people don't realize is that the best writers of us, the cops who can string sentences together in a report according to not just rules of grammar but the rules of how these reports should be made, are the ones who go the furthest in the departments. At the LAPD, the ones who had to rewrite their text constantly and had reports that came back with mistakes never rose far without support and a little bit of grandstanding from the higher-ups.

When I get to the podium with the lights and cameras pointing at me, I can't help but feel nervous. I focus on my report and tell myself to slow down my breathing.

My words have to be deliberate with a show of support and strength. But most of all, I have to be confident that yes, we will solve this murder.

I present the information that we know. Full names, ages, occupations. I mention that their daughter, Madison, nineteen years old, had gone missing three weeks ago.

Initially, it was suspected that she was staying with friends, but she has not been heard from since and her younger sister had filed a missing person's report with us. Everyone listens quietly. Afterward is a time for questions.

"What do you mean she wasn't reported missing earlier? Isn't three weeks a long time?" someone asks.

"She's nineteen years old. She went to community college here in the valley, but adults have the right to leave. There was some strife and issues of conflict with her parents, and that's why she was staying with friends for the weekend. She had a fight with her mom, but what was particularly strange, according to her sister, was that she never got back to her. And that's something that never happened."

"So why wasn't she reported missing earlier?"

"Because families are messy," I say. "Because they wanted to believe that she might have just taken off, which is still a possibility. But given the fact that both of her parents were found murdered in such a brutal way, at this point, we are looking for her and we are taking her disappearance very seriously."

Arms fly into the air, but I shake my head. "We're not taking any more questions at this time. That is all that I have to share with you."

"Is there any way the youngest daughter is a suspect in her parents' death?" someone yells.

I'm tempted to answer but I bite my tongue. The lieutenant told me not to address this question, in particular. I've given it plenty of my own thought.

I've come to the conclusion that, no, Franny had nothing to do with the death of her parents.

Now, her sister, on the other hand, I am not so sure about.

"You ready to go interview neighbors?" Will asks as soon as I'm done.

"Yeah, sure," I say, deciding to just power through the day despite the beginnings of a terrible headache. "Let me just use the bathroom and I'll meet you out front. We can take the same car."

On the way over, he asks me about the reunion, and I tell him about how nice it was to see everyone, glossing over the big story. Will and I are close friends, but I still feel a little uneasy telling him about what happened all those years ago.

My goal is to do some more preliminary work on the Kelsey Hall case tonight after I get home from working on this. Luckily, Will has always been an expert at organization, and he has a whole plan of who to talk to, when, and in what order.

"A couple of the neighbors were quite outgoing and interested. They called me up, made reports so I'd like to stop by there first," he says, pulling out his notebook and going through the names as I drive.

"Did you put out an all-points bulletin on Madison?" I ask.

He nods. This way all the cops in the state will be notified to be looking for her in what she was last known to be wearing.

"What about security cameras?" I ask.

"They hung them up apparently about a week before this happened, but never connected them. They weren't very technologically advanced as Franny put it. Not into "all those gadgets."

"What do you think this has to do with?"

"I'm not sure. I just hope that some of the neighbors saw something, but it seems doubtful."

I know exactly why he suspects that to be the case. The nearest property is almost a mile away. "The neighbors had cameras set up though," Will says. "I saw them."

"Let's hope they were working."

Will ends up being right. We talked to five neighbors, none of whom were home at the time. One of them did set up two cameras pointed outside of his double wide trailer.

His house sits on a property of almost two acres. He has a big pit bull, two horses, a pot belly pig, and a bunch of chickens. He says that someone had tried to steal his trampoline, the ones his kids play on out in the front yard. So he put up the cameras in case anyone else got any "funny ideas."

He is wearing a tank top and shorts with a drawstring around his Winnie the Pooh belly.

We request the recordings on his drive and he was happy to oblige, copying everything over to a USB while we waited in his cramped, overstuffed trailer with newspaper clippings of the JFK assassination all over the walls.

I ask him about it and he said that he recently watched a documentary and read the Stephen King book, 11/22/63, and became fascinated with the conspiracy that the government wasn't involved in the cover-up.

There's too much data to go through in this stuffy little room and the JFK researcher, as he prefers to be called, as opposed to conspiracy theorist, is eager for us to get out of here.

He heard nothing and didn't see anything of importance or what he thought was important on the tapes. Nothing was missing, but luckily he kept the files and it hasn't been long enough ago for them to get erased.

Back at the station, Will and I go through the recordings. The footage is a high quality Google Nest, but the camera is set up at a weird angle, focusing, obviously, on his property rather than the Dillard's'.

We click through to the day of the murders. Franny said that she saw them that morning and they were going to work in the office at home. She stopped by the station around noon. The recordings don't have anything of value, not really. We watch it again and again. Then I see a shadow.

"A car, perhaps," I say to Will.

He shrugs.

"Most likely. The perpetrators came in a vehicle and shot them when they were coming back into their property."

"But wait a second," I say. "Were they coming or going? It looked like the Dillards were out somewhere. Maybe the killers followed them?"

"*Killers?*" Will asks. "What makes you think there was more than one?"

"I don't know." I shake my head. "It just seems like a big job, executions, pulling teeth. Though who knows."

"If their teeth weren't pulled, I would say maybe, but we've got to talk to a profiler. That seems like something a solitary person would do."

I tap the pen on the counter nervously. Not sure where to go from here. When I look back up at Will, he's staring at me.

"I'm not going to talk to *him* about this," I say.

"You have to; this is for work."

"I'm not reaching out to my dad."

"He has years of experience with this type of thing. This is his job. Maybe he can point us in the right direction."

Will makes a lot of valid points, of course, but I'm frustrated because he knows my issues with my father. The last thing I want to do is to turn to him for help.

Unfortunately, I don't think I have much choice.

24

CHARLOTTE

My father and I meet at Tommy's, a casual American fare restaurant with lots of burgers and fries on the menu, but one that's trying to become a little bit more upscale. I get there early and he gets there right on time. He's punctual to a fault. Sometimes being places early and anticipating the meeting makes me feel like I'm more prepared, like I have the upper hand in something.

In this case, I'm not sure I have the upper hand in anything.

We have an early dinner together every other week. We usually have a standing date and time, but he was in DC for a while working and our schedule was adjusted accordingly.

I ask about his work, he asks about mine, and I can tell that he's restraining himself from not making me feel bad about not working for the FBI.

HE KNOWS nothing about the help that I need to ask for, but I'm sure that he will enjoy holding it over my head. No, that's not a particularly generous thing to say.

He will use it more like an opportunity to remind me what knowledge and wisdom I'm missing out on by not pursuing a career in the FBI.

But the truth is that I do need his help. He has heard about the double murder, but the missing daughter is news to him.

"There's something else that we haven't disclosed to the media," I say.

"Uh-huh." He nods, chomping at his Caesar salad, putting a generous amount of dressing on it.

"Their teeth were pulled," I say.

"The Dillard's?" he asks, perking up.

"It wasn't noticed right away, but someone took three teeth each from each one. We are doing an autopsy at this point and I guess we'll find out if it

was before or after they were shot. Likely after,"
I say.

Dad lifts up his eyes to meet mine.

"What are you asking me about Charlotte?" he says.

He's in his mid-sixties, fit, and still runs about five
miles a day. His hair is cut short, gray now, giving
him a distinguished look. He and I look surprisingly
alike and that's not a bad thing.

"Just trying to run the case by you, get any thoughts
you might have since you have so much experience,"
I say, being polite but staying firm.

I'm trying to hold onto authority. I'm not here
asking his advice as a daughter. I'm here more in
the capacity of a colleague, a professional.

"Well, the pulled teeth is not a good sign. It's a token
usually, as you know. Something to keep from a kill.
A memento."

"If it's a murder for hire, I have no idea why
someone would do that," I say. "If it's a murder for
pleasure, it makes perfect sense."

"But if it's a murder for pleasure, then why were
they shot? Executed?" Dad asks.

"That's what I'm thinking. They were killed too fast if it was someone who is a serial killer or on his way to becoming a serial killer, right?" I ask.

"I can look into it. See if we have any cases in a database that are at all a match for something like this. I don't know of anything off the top of my head," Dad volunteers.

"There's one other thing," I say. "This could be his first time."

"Of course, very possible," Dad agrees. "You checked cameras?"

"There's a neighbor with some cameras set up. We're still going through the evidence. I also have no idea if this is connected to the missing sister somehow, but it would be highly coincidental that their daughter goes missing and then three weeks later they end up dead, right? I mean, what is the likelihood of all that happening to the same family?"

"It's a lot of tragedy." He nods.

"You're not going to help me with this?" I ask.

"I said I would," Dad says dismissively. I pick up my fries, suddenly not very hungry.

"Look, I came here to talk to you about this. This is something big that I'm working on," I say. "I thought you could offer some expertise." "And I will. Do you want me to tell you what I think right here and right now?"

I nod.

"Okay. Well, just off the top of my head," Dad says, leaning back in the booth, "one direction is that he is a serial killer in the works. He committed the murders impulsively. He wanted to take a token. A memento as I had said but it wasn't planned."

"It wasn't sloppy either," I say, "there's not much evidence."

"Just because there's not much evidence doesn't mean that the person's an expert. On the other hand, it could be a hit for hire. You said that they were doing someone's audits. Tax stuff. It could be business related."

"The teeth make a lot less sense then," I point out.

"Yes. I would have to agree. A business dispute is usually just an execution. Nothing more."

"So, any advice?" I say after a very long pause.

"What do *you* think?" Dad says, putting his fork down, showing that he's done with lunch for good.

"I'm going to investigate the business angle, of course, but it's hard to tell. The teeth are really throwing me off. They seem either to be something very personal or someone very sinister and stark like a serial killer in the making, like you said," I point out. "Whenever I think it's one thing, it's maybe the other and then where does the missing sister fit in?"

"The other one's alive?" he asks.

"Yeah. She's the one that reported her missing."

"The parents didn't?"

"No." I give him a quick rundown of what we know so far. He taps his fingers on the table.

"This is a hard one," he says. "None of the facts are lining up. I'm not quite sure."

Our words linger in the air as we consider the case. He looks at me and then suddenly I notice him watching me, his eyes narrowing. He runs his hands through his hair and gives me a smile.

"What? Why are you looking at me like that?" I ask.

"I'm just proud of you," Dad says the words that I've heard only on a very few occasions in my whole life.

"Really?"

He nods. "Just didn't think that you had this in you."

"What do you mean?" I ask.

"It's good to see you at work, working on something meaningful."

For once I want to add something, but I bite my tongue. He's being nice. Trying to say something kind.

"Thank you," I say.

I wait for him to add that had I gotten into the FBI, I'd have more of an opportunity to pursue this kind of work and investigation, but he surprises me by keeping his mouth shut.

Instead, when the check arrives, Dad simply pays it and tells me that I should reach out to Shelly.

"She hasn't heard from you for a while and she misses you. You've got to come over for dinner. Do a whole family thing," he says. "I'll get your siblings out as well."

"Okay," I agree. "I'd love to."

25

CHARLOTTE

R ight before leaving, Dad reminds me that his lifetime achievement award dinner got postponed, but he'll send me the details. I promise to be there unless something comes up.

He seems a little bit disappointed, but I know that he of all people should understand what it's like doing this job. I can't even remember now how many special occasions and holidays got postponed because he had to work. Dad didn't even make it to my high school graduation because there was a small break in the Badlands serial killer case.

I have a little bit of time. Not wanting to put it off any longer, I decide to visit Madison's friends, the last place where she was seen. This visit is unannounced, the precise kind I like to make, to put additional pressure on people who may have something to admit.

I pull into a gentrifying neighborhood. On one side of the street is a rebuilt, updated 1950's house with twelve foot shrubs for additional privacy. The one next door has recently been sold and is in the process of construction.

The one across the street is dilapidated. It's not falling down completely, but has definitely seen better days. It's a one story, looks to be about 1200 square feet with a broad but almost nonexistent lawn and dried up plants out front.

After parking on the street in front of the wooden garage door that swings straight up instead of folding, I make my way up the cracked driveway. It takes someone on the other side a little bit to answer.

"Mesquite County Sheriff's Department, open up," I say, using my loudest police knock.

"We'll be right there," a female voice mumbles.

It could be either Colby or Meredith, the two who are officially renting the house. I've done a little bit of research on them on social media and I know who's who.

From Franny, I know that Colby's boyfriend, Tyler Alhous, is living here as well. Colby Durango opens the door. Her blonde hair is pulled up into a loose bun. She's wearing a tank top cut off at the midriff and high waisted jeans. I wouldn't be able to tell otherwise, but in this particular outfit, she looks pregnant.

I introduce myself and show her my badge and she welcomes me inside. The place is dark. None of the lights are on and it is quite hot, like the inside of a furnace.

"Your air not working?"

"No," she says. "Actually the electricity's out. We couldn't pay the bill and the place heats up like crazy. Come, we can sit outside."

I sit in a plastic, rickety, white chair with cracking armrests and Colby sits across from me. When I ask her how far along she is, she says six months and tells me that Tyler's just taking a shower, but he'll be out soon. "Luckily it's not that cold anymore, but the heat is getting to me, too."

"Will you be able to get it turned on?" I ask.

"Yeah, I think so. Meredith's supposed to get paid soon. We're pooling our money together."

"That's good," I say and get right to the point.

I tell her that I'm here to ask about Madison, what their relationship was like the last time she saw her, anything that she could help me with. She looks distressed, sad, and glances away for a second.

"When she left, everything was normal," Colby finally starts. "It was like any other day. She sometimes came here for the weekends just to hang out. I mean, I saw her at work all the time, but her parents were getting to her. She was upset with her whole situation. She didn't want to be at that community college. She wanted to go to some good school. She wasn't even doing well there. She wasn't studying. She was just depressed."

"Is the pay good at the Desert Willow Country Club?"

"Yeah, it depends," Colby says.

Tyler comes out with three glasses of ice water, which are greatly appreciated. Colby immediately presses hers to her forehead and neck. And, just at that moment, I realize that the umbrella's not even open to provide some shade. I start to reach up to get it up, but Tyler beats me to it.

"The pay's good if you flirt with the golfers and you act all submissive and friendly. It's not so good if you're pregnant. It's not so good if you stop paying attention to how you present yourself."

"What do you mean by that?" I ask.

"Well, when Madison dolled herself up, washed her hair, put on the fake lashes, makeup, and smiled a lot and went out of her way, it was okay. I mean, they don't pay crap. It's below minimum wage, but the tips were good. It really depends on the tipper and what kind of day they had at the golf course. When Madison stopped paying as much attention to her appearance, stopped washing her hair, stopped wearing makeup, just stopped going out of her way to be nice, things got kind of rough."

"I'm so sorry," I say without thinking.

"It's fine," Colby says. "She was helping us out with money, too, because I have all these doctors' appointments and they're really expensive. I don't have any insurance. I mean, I had it and then I lost it when I changed jobs and so it's just... I still want to go to all the ultrasounds and I pay out of pocket mostly just to make sure the baby's okay. Madison was helping a lot with that. And now…"

Tears well up in her eyes.

"What do you think could have happened to her?"

"I can't really say."

Tyler doesn't add much, but I can see how caring he is with his girlfriend. They've been together since high school and the baby is wanted. Not exactly planned, but there is no question that they are going to keep it.

"Madison is going to be a good godmother. And Meredith, too," she says, taking a sip of her glass.

She doesn't use the past tense. She's holding on to hope.

"Hey, did Madison happen to leave any of her electronics around? Phone, iPad, computer, anything at all?"

26

MADISON

I'm leaving tonight.

No one knows and it's probably better this way. My friends think that I'm going to be at work, but I took a whole week off. They wouldn't approve. In this day and age, there's no way that you could talk to someone online for years and have it be anything but a fraud, especially if you've never video chatted before.

I've seen the show *Catfish*, but I'm trying to be safe. I want to meet him.

I took time off from work because it's going to take me a bit to get there. I'm taking my car with me because it's a long trip. I've never been up there before.

James and I have talked online for five years.

We met in a chat group, for people who like *My Little Pony*. I first started watching it with my little sister and thought it was just a kids show. But the more I watched, the more I liked it. Franny would wake up in the mornings to binge the show and I just joined in.

The more I watched, the more I realized that the show is both for kids and adults. It has so many layers of meaning. Each season has different lessons and even Lampoon's American 1920s Imperialism and Soviet communism.

As time passed, I got involved with the fandom by watching songs on YouTube, looking at fan art and reading fanfic. That's when I met James. I went on the *My Little Pony* subreddit and later the chatroom the night that Mom and Dad had one of their many fights and talks about divorce and I just needed to be somewhere else.

James was a big fan, too, and that's how we first connected. He was a friend at first, nothing more, and we talked about anything and everything. It wasn't until two years later that it occurred to me, to even exchange photos with him.

He is a year older than I am, and he lives with his mom. We each have our own insecurities. I am about thirty pounds heavier than I want to be, eating junk food, to try to deal with my unhappy home life. He said that he doesn' look the way he wants to either.

Instead of sharing a fake picture of himself, James said he'd rather tell me what he looks like.

"Dark hair, pimples, *doughy* complexion."

That's the word he used, and I remember because I had to look it up.

There was a time when I used to save every one of our extremely long text message conversations.

But then I started to take screenshots of snippets, saving the parts where he shared parts of himself and told me he loved me.

Over the years, we've had relationships with other people.

Sometimes we'd talk often and other times we wouldn't talk more than once every couple weeks.

But he was always there when I broke up with a friend, when I broke up with a guy, when someone stood me up.

I'm at a crossroads now. James has just broken up with his girlfriend and is single again after a year.

If I want to meet him, it has to be now or never.

Why not take a chance?

I LOVE DRIVING MY CAR, a 2015, bright blue Toyota Prius . I turn the music up loud as I drive and listen to the hum of the freeway. I've never driven this far by myself.

Three hours east to Needles, California, is where James lives. I told him that I was coming, but he didn't seem to believe me. He did give me a number to call, and this will be our first conversation over the phone.

I listen to the last bars of an Ariana Grande song and then turn off Spotify on my phone. Going seventy miles an hour, I dial his number. Perhaps I should have called him earlier, and I have some regrets, but it is what it is.

Better now than later.

I'm driving deep into the desert, no signs here, just sand, and shrubs, and creosote bushes all around. The sky is as big and wide as the entire world without a single cloud obscuring its blueness. That's just the way that I love it.

"James?"

A man answers. It definitely belongs to a man who is not very old. Of course, it's a concern that I've had that he doesn't look the way that he has described himself to look.

"How are you doing, Madison?" he asks.

I can feel the trepidation, uncertainty in his voice.

"Are you really coming to see me?"

"Yes, I am," I say. "Can you hear that?" I put the phone out next to the window. "That's the road out there. I'll be at your place in two hours."

"I can't believe you're coming here. I can't believe we haven't done this before. What about your work?" he asks.

We've been texting all day, every day, but somehow, speaking to him in person changes everything. The closeness is difficult to describe. No words on paper can match it. And now I regret more than anything that we haven't video chatted before.

"Will you keep me company?" I ask. "This is our first conversation, after all."

"I know. I can't wait to see you."

As we talk, I realize that James sounds exactly like he does in his texts. It's like the words coming out of his mouth are verbatim and a perfect match to the thoughts that he has sent.

He asks me about work, about my friends. He knows all of them by name and what they're like. I even sent him a few pictures. He's taking classes at the community college in Needles, just like I am.

Needles, California, is where he grew up, a resort town on the western banks of the Colorado River, near the borders of California, Arizona, and Nevada. He works in one of those towns at the poker tables in a casino.

"Why haven't we ever video chatted before?" I ask, after a little bit of a lull in conversation about the day to day.

"I don't know. Remember we wanted to at first, and then we thought it would be more romantic if we met each other without having seen each other first?"

"Yeah, but it's dangerous, you know? What if all of this connection that we've had over text doesn't match? There's a lot to be said for physical attraction."

"I know, but I have no doubt that I'm going to love you and that you are hot as hell," James jokes. "But I do have to tell you something I probably should have told you earlier."

I sink deeper into my seat, my pulse quickening.

A secret. Of course. Probably one of many.

Why not? Everybody's a fake version of themselves online, right? "I'm a little older than I told you. I'm not twenty."

"How old are you?" I ask.

He hesitates again. "Twenty-five."

"Five years isn't too bad, I guess," I say. "But you shouldn't have lied."

"I lied when we first got started talking," he says. "It was embarrassing. What was I doing in a *My Little Pony* chatroom? I didn't want you to think that I was some creep picking up a young girl. I just didn't have any friends or interests, and I needed to talk to someone."

"Yeah, I know," I say. "So if you're twenty-five, then what else is untrue?"

"What do you mean?" James asks.

I wrap my hands firmer around the steering wheel. I'm wearing dark sunglasses, but the sun is still too bright, forcing me to squint at the road. There's no one in front of me, but there are a few passing trucks coming the other way.

Otherwise, it's just me, alone here, driving into the unknown. "Did you go to college?"

"I still am," he says. "I'm just not taking the four classes like I told you. I took a semester off, and most of the time, one class was all I could manage. I just needed a lot of off time between my full-time work at the casino, paying for my mom's medical bills. It's a lot. And yeah, I probably take a lot more time off than I should, but I'm just mentally spent, you know?" It's a phrase he has used often, *mentally spent*, exhausted, tired.

"I'm not sure what to say," I reply when he asks me if I'm still there. I let the silence go on a little too long again. "You lied to me and I'm just not sure what to do with that. Do you even look like you said you do? Do you even have this name?"

"People call me Jim, but I prefer James. My last name is the same. I have a social media account. You can look me up if you want to. Then you'll know what I look like."

I'm tempted to pull over right here, right now by the side of the road and do exactly that.

"I can tell you the handle. It's my private account with friends and family that I know directly. I never told you about it because, I don't know, I keep my online life sort of separate. And you never told me about yourself either."

"I know. I'm sorry about that," I say.

After a little while, I tell him that I have to go. I want to talk more, but the silences are unbearable. I need time to think.

"Tell me one thing?" James asks. "Are you still heading over here?"

"Yeah."

"You're still going to come today?"

"Yeah."

"Do you want to come to my house? I can send you the address."

"No." I shake my head. I'm not ready for that. "Let's meet somewhere public, like a Starbucks or diner, anywhere."

"Okay. Starbucks it is. I'll send you the address of one nearby," he says. Then James adds, "I love you."

"I'll talk to you later," I say, cutting him off, not reciprocating on purpose.

After I hang up, I don't put the music back on. Instead, I listen to the lull of the road. I'm still heading there, and I still haven't looked at his Facebook account.

I don't know if I believe everything he says anymore, but I don't know if I think that he's lying.

I see a sign for Needles, California, 150 miles away, and I drive past it, hoping that everything will be okay when I get there and when I find out the truth.

27

CHARLOTTE

C olby looks around the house and together with Tyler, they find Madison's iPad under a pile of magazines on the coffee table.

"Yeah, this is definitely hers," Colby says. "I just got a new one, but my other one is charging in the room."

"Would you mind if I look at it?" I ask, and they let me take it. When I turn it on, Colby tells me the code to get in. It's her birthday. Of course, it is.

"I'm going to take this back to the lab," I tell them.

"Thanks. Please give me a call if you find anything at all. I hope she's okay," Colby says, before giving me a warm hug.

I look through the iPad myself first in the station's parking lot. I check her emails, reading through the last couple and then scrolling. There's a bunch that arrived after her disappearance, but I scroll down to that weekend and check for anything suspicious.

Nothing really jumps out at me.

I check the browser history, and much to my surprise, I see that she searched for Needles, California, on the map and how long the trip would take.

"Hmm," I say quietly to myself, and then head over to the messages.

As I click on them, they quickly load, syncing with her iCloud account, and that's when I stumble upon a treasure trove.

Someone named James with a Heart emoji next to his name has a whole string of messages. Madison and James talk about her sister, her parents, and how much they love one another. They share no pictures, at least not in the last few weeks prior to her disappearance.

A quick search on Google reveals a phone number registered to James Bensinger with an address in Needles, California.

I search his name on Instagram and it shows a private account, but when I put it into Facebook, I find a close-up of a young guy with dark piercing eyes.

The privacy settings are relatively open and I access some photos and information on the about section. He's attending Needles Community College and working at a casino. There are pictures of him having fun at the pool, lounging in the Colorado River on an inflatable raft, and generally living the life of a twenty-five-year-old.

The last update is from April 1st.

She's coming. I'm finally going to meet her!

A few replies appear below.

"Who?"

"Who is she?"

But no one gets a reply.

I go back to the text messages and look at the date of the last one, April 2nd.

"Crap," I say to myself. If they were going to meet up, that was the last time that they communicated.

Are they together, and that's why they're not texting each other anymore? But why didn't he reply on Facebook?

He could just not be active. He could have not checked his posts, not replied. But he could have also been involved in Madison's disappearance. What if they met and she didn't like him? What if he didn't appreciate that?

Despite talking for a long time, they are certainly still strangers.

A number of messages are about how they've never seen each other in the flesh and don't have any pictures of one another.

This I find baffling, but they call it *romantic*.

I drop the iPad off at the cyber-tech guy who's stuffing his face with a sandwich at lunch.

"After you finish here, would you mind taking a look at this?" I catch him up on what I've found so far and how it relates to my case.

He mumbles, "Yes," as I hand him the iPad wrapped in an evidence bag.

I find the lieutenant and fill him in on what I found out and he begrudgingly agrees to let me go to Needles.

"I'll go now. Tonight," I offer.

He shakes his head no. "It's already getting late. You'll have to pay for a hotel room. Just go tomorrow morning. The station will be open there during normal hours and you can fill them in on what's going on."

I can do a part of this over the phone, video conferencing, all that modern jazz, but I have an address for James Bensinger and I want to be there to talk to him, or whoever answers the door.

A local deputy from Needles with no knowledge of the case might mess things up. I don't want to tip him off, and if that happens, I want to be there to make sure that everything goes smoothly.

I spend the night restlessly, my thoughts going over anything and everything that might have happened. I have no idea whether Madison's disappearance has anything to do with her parent's double murder. But this shouldn't take more than half a day, full day at most, and they have Will and the rest of the department working on the murder investigations.

If Madison ran away, she has no idea what happened to her parents and she deserves to know. I want to find her and bring her back, but what if something bad happened to her? What if she's not there?

The following morning, I pack a small bag. I have no intentions of staying overnight, but I hate being caught places without some of the comforts of home; mostly electronics and charging cables, my notebook, and some other things.

Just in case I do have to stay in a motel room, I bring my pillow, the one that I got into the habit of traveling with ever since I had problems with my neck a few years ago. I also throw the eyeliner pencil, foundation, mascara, dry shampoo, a stick of deodorant, a toothbrush, a pair of underwear, and a top into a striped weekend bag.

When I toss it into the front seat of my Toyota, a car pulls up and Dylan Ferreira comes out holding a paper bag with a Palm Valley Bagels logo.

"Hey. Where are you going?" he asks.

"What are you doing here?" I say, slamming the door of the passenger seat shut.

"Just wanted to come by and bring some breakfast. Tried to call you a few times."

"Yeah, and I didn't call you back. You tried to text me, too," I point out.

"Yeah, I just thought you got busy."

"Maybe I did." I smile. "Maybe I was just rejecting you in a polite way."

"By ghosting me?" Dylan shifts his weight.

Dressed in jeans and a slim fit T-shirt, he flashes his megawatt white smile that stands out against his tan skin. He has dark curly hair that is a little too long, but in that utterly sexy way, and he broadens his shoulders widely, pushing his Ray-Ban sunglasses to the top of his head. His blue eyes sparkle in the sunlight, and he gives me a little smirk.

"What's the matter? You've never been ghosted before?" I ask.

"Most definitely. Just thought I'd give it another shot."

"Honestly, wish I could," I say, "but I've got to go. Taking a bit of a drive."

"Where to?"

"Needles. It's about three hours from here. I have to interview a possible suspect. Long story."

"How about a summary?" Dylan asks.

"Okay, fine. But I've got to get some more stuff from the house, so you're welcome to follow me in."

As he walks behind me, I tell him that the missing girl that I've been looking for has a secret online boyfriend that she's never met, and she went out to meet him the day that she disappeared.

"That's ominous," he says.

I nod. "Yeah. It's not the best."

Looking around the foyer, I grab my purse, try to think if I should take anything else, and then head to the kitchen and refill my big metal insulated water bottle.

"So, you can't even do a quick breakfast bite?" he asks as I usher him out the door.

"No, sorry. I'd love to, but I really have to go. It's a long drive and at this point, it's already going to be eleven by the time I get there."

"I have an idea," Dylan offers, following behind me.

"Sure. Uh-huh," I mumble.

"What if I were to come with you?"

"What do you mean?" I turn around.

"Well, you're going for the day, right? What if I come with you and we kind of have our date on the ride?"

My lips turn up at the corners and it takes physical pressure to make it go away.

"Well, if the date doesn't go well, we're going to be stuck in the car for the whole day," I point out.

"Yeah. I guess that's just a risk we're going to have to take."

I bite my lower lip, thinking. "I really have to go."

"Can I come?" he asks again.

"I'm not going to stop you," I say and smile broadly as he jumps in the passenger seat, tossing my weekend bag in the back.

28

CHARLOTTE

It would be a lie to say that my heart doesn't beat a little faster sitting next to Dylan, especially given the way that he invited himself on this trip. With anyone else, I probably would have said no, but there's something about him that makes me take pause.

We drive for a while and he asks me about the case. I fill him in with as many details as I can, appreciative of the fact that he used to be a detective in San Francisco and may offer some insight. He listens carefully. I can tell that he's a little bit taken aback by the fact that Mr. and Mrs. Dillard's teeth were pulled.

"Are you sure it happened during the murders?" I roll my eyes in his direction and he waves his hand. "Yeah, I know, I know. It's crazy."

"It just seems strange," he says. "Do you have people investigating their accounting business?"

"Yeah. Will's working on that now. I will be as well. Just had this lead on Madison and hope against hope, I guess, that I'll find her there."

"Have you found many missing persons?" he asks.

I nod.

"Surprisingly, yes. I mean, television shows, that kind of thing will have you believe that people are missing forever, but a lot of them are found. A lot of them are runaways or they leave of their own volition. Madison can't exactly be a runaway, as you know. She's nineteen years old and now, finally, there's a piece of the puzzle. She was going to see her boyfriend. One she never met, mind you."

"You think that's stupid?" he asks.

I nod. "Don't you? In this day and age, especially given the video conferencing software that everyone has access to. I mean, why not FaceTime? It just doesn't make any sense."

"When did they meet?" Dylan asks.

"I don't know exactly. They were talking for a while. The last message was like a year ago, but I found a whole bunch of screenshots from a couple years back. She kept some of the best ones, I guess. Their deeper conversations about life and love."

"That's sweet, isn't it?" Dylan asks.

"Of course it's sweet. But it's also stupid and irresponsible. She has no idea who she's meeting. She didn't check his name. I know that for a fact because she said so herself. Can you believe it?"

"Not everybody's a detective, Charlotte. I'm sure that prior to inviting me on this trip, you looked me up, right? Know me frontward and backward? My background?"

I bite my lower lip.

"No, you didn't, did you?"

"We met once. Besides, Will vouched for you."

"I haven't seen Will in years. I mean, we were friends, but still."

"Is there something I should worry about?"

"No, but my point is that you can't expect everybody to behave like cops. Even cops. It's probably not a great idea for you to take a trip with an almost stranger who has kind of a shoddy record that you even know about with the police department, right?"

Dylan's joking, leaning back, being cool.

"You think you're just so charming and no one can resist your advances, right?" I say, hating the fact that I'm falling for it, all this bravado and confidence. It can make a person appear to be such a jerk, and yet, at the same time, completely irresistible. Dylan fell into the latter category.

"Look, the only point I'm trying to make here," Dylan says, throwing up his arms and leaning a little bit closer to me, "is that she's in love, and people do stupid things when they're in love. Heck, you don't even have to be in love. You could just have a crush on someone…Like me."

"What do you mean?" I ask.

"Well, coming here, I thought I would just bring you some bagels and cream cheese. We'd have a nice little breakfast, get to know each other. I did not expect to be jumping in the car with you and driving three hours each way to work on a case just to get a little bit of time. It's probably not great. I mean, if you turn out to be terribly boring, self-involved, arrogant, and all the other boring descriptors of a terrible date, I'd have no choice but to stick out the whole day with you, and it's one of my only days off. But back in your driveway, I was just there and I felt like we connected. Like, sure, let's go for it. If it's terrible, lesson learned. But what if it's not? What if you're fun? What if we click?"

I nod, knowing exactly what he means.

"Being a cop gives you this terrible view of the world, like everyone's out to get you, like everyone has bad intentions," Dylan continues. "But that's a small part of the population. And yeah, maybe it's stupid for a nineteen-year-old girl to do that, but she did talk to James for years. Maybe she knew him better than we think she did."

"She never saw his face," I say. "Or his real social media page. What if he's fifty years old?"

"And what if he's exactly who he says he is?" Dylan says. "What if she's there with him, just hanging out, not answering her phone?"

"Well, I guess we'll find out." I nod. "And also, I really hope you're right. It'd be great if she were alive and well and had nothing to do with her parents' murder."

"But?" he asks.

"But, I can't help but think otherwise."

"Like there's a big conspiracy?" Dylan asks.

I nod. "Yeah, it kind of warps your mind, doesn't it? Doing this job? Is that why you don't work anymore? Is that why you quit?"

He sits back in his seat and looks out the window.

The golden yellow desert stretches out in all directions under the bright blue sky. The vista is breathtaking, dotted with creosote bushes, an occasional Joshua tree, and a whole lot of sand.

"It's beautiful out here," he says. "Isn't it?"

He's changing the topic. But if he doesn't want to talk about it, I'm not going to press. We all have secrets and things we've done that we're not proud of.

"My partner got shot," he says after a long pause, looking at the horizon. "Ambushed, really. We were told to be at a certain location. It was supposed to be a crack den. It was, except there were people there waiting for us, like they'd been tipped off. I managed to get out, but he got shot. I didn't have enough firepower, and not a day goes by that I don't think about him and what I could have and should have done."

"They were waiting for you?" I ask.

"Yeah. Four of them, and two of them were cops."

29

CHARLOTTE

When I glance over at him, his eyes don't meet mine. He looks out into the distance. For a second, I don't think that I heard him right.

"What do you mean, two of them were cops?" I ask.

"Exactly that. They worked in vice. My partner suspected that they were getting kickbacks. They were dealing meth and crack and who knows what else. They were selling drugs, working with the gang in the neighborhood. We had our suspicions. We trailed this one dealer one day, totally low level, nothing special. We didn't think we'd find anything. And then, there was the other cop, Lansen, at the motel, meeting up."

We drive further into the vastness. His voice is low and quiet. The creosote bushes rush past us.

"What are you trying to tell me, Dylan?" I ask. "Are you trying to say that there's something going on? That you were set up?"

"I *am* telling you that," he says, looking away toward the horizon. "Two cops set me up. They were crooked, into a lot of illegal crap. We followed them, saw them at the motel meeting with one of the biggest dealers in the area. They were carrying a suitcase out to their car, which I later found out held a bunch of cash. Kickbacks. They were corrupt as hell."

"So, what happened?" I ask.

"We had to decide whether to go to Internal Affairs or handle the problem ourselves."

"And?"

"IA could have gotten us killed. We had no idea who they were friends with and which higher-ups had their back. We planned to investigate to find out exactly how deep this went in the department and who was paying them off. We wanted to catch them on video so that the evidence was irrefutable. But then my partner got killed."

"What happened?" I ask.

He shakes his head. "I'll tell you some other time. This isn't exactly a great story for a first date."

I reach over, grab his hand, and give him a slight squeeze.

"Thanks for telling me," I say. "You can open up to me about anything."

"We'll see." He smiles.

"I have a feeling you don't trust people easily."

"What makes you say that?" Dylan jokes. "I mean, look at us, we just met, it's our first date and I tell you the worst thing that ever happened in my career."

"Yes, but I have a feeling that that's because of Will."

"Will is a standup guy," Dylan says. "He was one of my closest friends. I don't know how he's still doing all this work, or you for that matter. Except maybe Mesquite County Sheriff's Department is a little bit easier to maneuver in, to be on the right side of the law."

"You think it's just San Francisco or the big cities?"

"Big cities have their problems. A lot of politics, a lot more cops to try to take some shortcuts. Tell me about LA, what was it like?"

"Not exactly a similar experience I admit, but it wasn't the best. It had its perks. I liked the high-paced work and everything else that went along with it, but I disagreed with a lot of the management policies and there wasn't much I could do about it, but you're right, let's not talk about work right now unless you wanna tell me about firefighting."

"Firefighting is actually pretty fun if you like high adrenaline and living on the edge. It's a nice way to pass the time."

"Yes, that's what I hear," I say sarcastically.

"Are you serious?" He shrugs.

"Yes, maybe I'm a maniac. I've always liked fire. Now, I get to extinguish it for a living, but mostly, I just like the camaraderie. Everybody has the same goal. There are very clear good guys and bad guys. The fire's the bad guy, someone who started it, nature, whatever. I don't have a family, not many friends here besides you and Will, so I don't mind the hours. It keeps me busy, so to speak."

"What are your hours? How much do you work?"

"Right now, not so much. The usual twelve hour days, that kind of thing, on-off, but it's not fire season yet, as you know. That's going to start in the summertime, and then I can be sent anywhere, really. Up and down California. There are going to be a lot of fires as always. Maybe San Diego, San Bernardino Mountains, Malibu, all the usual suspects."

He gives me a wink.

"Have you ever lost anyone there?"

"Yes, a few men, a woman as well. It's very tragic, but I like fighting a natural force. You have to watch your back, but not in the same way that you do with people, you know what I mean?"

I nod. "Exactly."

The rest of the way, the conversation waxes and wanes over various topics. We talk about music and movies. We don't really have much in common.

I discover that he is obsessed with Roman history, Hannibal military campaigns, likes to listen to all the podcasts and read all the books. He even started taking online classes to refresh his knowledge of Latin of all languages. He studied it in college.

"You know that's a dead language, right?" I say. "I mean, if you're going to learn a new language, don't you want to learn one where you can communicate with people who actually speak it?"

"You'd be surprised how nice it is to learn a language that no one speaks." Dylan laughs and I can't help but smile.

After a little while, I wonder how it is that he's single. He's personable, attractive. Let's also be frank, he's fit and easy on the eyes with a good attitude and a great sense of humor. I find it hard to believe that no woman has gotten a hold of him quite yet. Unless, of course, there is something wrong with him.

"You drive fast, you know. At this rate, we'll be there in two and a half hours unless some overworked police officer pulls you over."

"Probably not, though." I give him a wink. "You worried about your safety or something else?"

"I think I'd just like to spend the extra half hour with you."

He gives me a nod and I can't help but beam. I lift my foot off the accelerator and decrease my speed a good twenty miles an hour.

"How about this?" I say, pointing to the odometer. "Is sixty-five good for you?"

"Perfect," Dylan says.

"Can I ask you something?" I ask. He nods. "What's your situation?"

"My situation?"

"Yes, I mean, you seem like a nice guy, easy on the eyes. Why hasn't anyone snagged you yet?"

"No, someone did." He nods.

My face drops. "You've got to be kidding me. You're married?"

"No, I'm not," he says, looking at the odometer as I start to increase our speed close to ninety.

"Slow down there, speed demon. No, I'm not married. I used to be. My wife died."

"You said you were divorced."

"I lied. I didn't want to go into it."

"Oh, wow, I'm sorry."

"We were married for fifteen years. Right out of college we were together exclusively, best friends."

"Oh, I'm so sorry, what happened?" I ask, secretly hoping that it wasn't some long-drawn-out illness because I know how painful those can be.

"Car accident. It was so stupid," he says. "A drunk driver hit her at the intersection."

"I'm sorry," I whisper. "You never had kids?"

He shakes his head no.

"I worked a lot of hours. She was a doctor, she worked plenty as well. We'd actually just started talking about having one. It was getting to be sort of a now or never situation and we had to talk about it. She is two years older than me. Was," Dylan corrects himself.

He pauses for a moment to collect his thoughts.

"That happened a couple of months before all the stuff with vice went down and my partner got shot. It was a tough year, but I did what I always do, buried myself in work. Then had a bit of a breakdown. Just couldn't do it anymore. One day I went to work and walked out on my shift. I finally managed to force myself to call my lieutenant, but that was pretty much it."

"Did the break help?" I ask.

"It made things worse. I thought that I could just deal with it, work through it, but it was burnout and grief and everything all at once."

"I'm so sorry," I say.

"I don't know what kind of dates you've been going on, but this is getting a little intense," Dylan admits. "I mean, I didn't expect to go into my whole life story when I got into this car this morning, and look, we didn't even eat our bagels."

He grabs the bag.

"Yes, a bagel sounds nice," I say, my stomach rumbling.

He laughs."Really? Is that you?"

I nod. "Yes, I guess I'm a little hungry."

"Can I put some cream cheese on yours?" he offers.

I nod and watch as he carefully dips the plastic knife into the tiny container and smears it carefully on the bagel. He makes little waves all around and I watch him move ever so smoothly lifting his eyes only once to give me a wink.

"We're almost there," I say, pointing to the sign for Needles, five miles. "Thanks for coming with me."

I smile at him when he hands me half of my bagel. It had been toasted a few hours back and has gotten a little soggy sitting in the bag.

Nevertheless, it's the best thing I've tasted in a really long time.

30

CHARLOTTE

We head straight to James Bensinger's address. Dylan brings up the option of heading to the police station and letting them know what we are doing, which is the courteous thing to do, but I figured instead of asking for permission, I'd rather ask for forgiveness.

"This is going to be nothing but a casual talk," I promise him. "I just want to see when the last time was that James saw Madison or if she even made it here."

"What if he is the one who's responsible for her death?" Dylan asks.

"No one is saying that she's dead," I point out.

"Yes, I know that, but you know that it's possible, right?"

"Of course, I do," I say. "I just don't want it to be that."

"No one does."

"Well, in any case, this will catch him by surprise. Me coming all this way. Maybe he'll say something that he doesn't mean to. You know how it works."

"Yes, the element of surprise is important, but he could be someone who clams up."

We go back and forth, but since this is my investigation, I decide to go ahead with it. A moment later, I believe that we arrive at a dusty middle-class community with one-story buildings, and at the end of the cul-de-sac, sits James Bensinger's house. It's not much to look at, but it's not particularly small or dilapidated either, just nondescript. The grass up front has dried up and no one has bothered to fix the sprinklers. There are two rickety cars parked out front, one with a smashed-in door, both are dusty and dirty.

I ask Dylan to wait in the car, but he says that he's coming with me. I don't protest. It's good to have backup.

The knock on the door is confident and strong, but it takes a few knocks before someone answers. A few minutes later, a man dressed in jeans and a tank top who looks like he just woke up stumbles toward the door. His eyes are bloodshot with deep circles underneath, but I don't smell any alcohol on his breath. He looks worn out.

"Excuse me, are you James Bensinger?"

"Yes," he mumbles. "What's this about?"

He doesn't look frightened, just annoyed with why I'm here. I introduce myself, but don't bother with Dylan.

"Mesquite County Sheriff's Department?"

He repeats my words back to me.

"Why are you here?"

"Well, we're looking for someone you were in contact with online, Madison Dillard."

He nods and suddenly looks down at the ground.

"Oh, no, did her parents report her missing? Is that why you're here?"

"Do you happen to know where she is?" I ask, avoiding his question.

"Madison!" he yells back into the house. "Maddie!"

A moment later, a woman appears in a bathrobe and leggings. Her hair is pulled up into a loose ponytail. A little bit of old makeup still lingers around her eyes. Holding an iPad, she pulls her earphone out of her ear and looks at me tilting her head.

"Oh my God, did my parents call the police? Are they serious?"

My mouth drops a little bit. She looks exactly like the girl on the Missing Person's poster. A lot less makeup, more relaxed, but the hair is colored and I can see the attitude. She drops her earbuds into the pocket of her bathrobe, shaking her head.

"I'm really sorry for wasting your time. You didn't have to come all the way over here."

"You're here. You're alive?" It comes out more like a question than a statement.

She nods. "Of course, I'm alive."

"Your family's been very worried about you," I say, trying to be careful with my words, not wanting to tell her more than absolutely necessary at this point.

"How did you find out about him?" she asks.

"Colby gave me your old iPad. Looks like you got another one."

"No, this is his. I forgot that one and kept kicking myself over it. How could I forget it? Anyway."

"So did you search it?" she asks.

"Yes, I did. That's how I traced you to this place."

"James and I just met in person."

"From your text messages, it seemed like you knew each other well."

"Yes, except what we looked like."

"Would you mind if I come in?" I ask.

"Yes, sure," James says, but Madison begins to protest.

"Look, I'm an adult. I know that I probably should have told my parents, but whatever. They know what it's like. My mom did practically the same thing. I should have told my sister, but I didn't, so whatever. It is what it is."

"Please," I say, "I really need to tell you something. It's very important."

THE NEWS that I have for Madison is difficult to deliver. I'm still in a little bit of shock at the fact that she's alive and unharmed, completely oblivious to what has happened to her family. In the low-ceilinged living room with very low light, I stand on the shag carpet and I tell Madison about her parents. She breaks down burying her face in

James's shoulder. Through the sobs, she keeps repeating, "No. No. No. This can't be happening. No, it's not true." It takes her a little bit before she's coherent again and answers my questions.

She sits on the edge of an overstuffed couch with her feet tucked under herself. James brings her a cup of tea and I open my notebook to take notes and set up the recorder on my phone. She confirms that she left that Sunday after she took off from Colby and Meredith's place. She tells me that she took a week off from work but then called in and said she needed more time off since she was enjoying James's company so much.

"They didn't mention that," I point out.

"They were just covering their butts. They essentially fired me," Madison says quietly. "It's fine because we were talking about me moving here. It's more affordable and there are always jobs at the casino.

"I figured that I can always get my job back if something goes wrong since they usually are kind of low on employees anyway."

"Is there a reason why you never told your parents?" I ask.

"I was angry with them. We had a big fight right before I went to Colby and Meredith's. They were just refusing to understand what I was going through."

"Which was?" I ask.

"Something bad happened my last year of high school. I was on a date with this guy and he refused to take no for an answer. He forced himself on me. I don't want to go into the details," Madison says, looking away with tears in her eyes, "but that's why I didn't want to go to college. I was just so dead inside. I mean, I got all of these acceptances and I was scared. I wanted to stay in my room and hide from the world and--"

"Your parents didn't understand that?" I ask.

"They said they did. But they didn't. The problem was that I kind of told them a little bit about it but not everything because I was embarrassed, because they didn't think that I should go on the date with him. It was late and it was irresponsible and it was just a big mess. We talked about me applying to four-year colleges again and going away to school and they were saying how I wasn't even doing well in the community college so how did I plan on getting in? They were right. I thought staying home would make it easier but it just made it so much more complicated."

She takes a deep breath and James squeezes her hand.

"The only thing that made sense at that point was talking to James and so I just wanted to meet him," Madison continues. "When I heard that he and his girlfriend had broken up, they were having problems for a while, I just decided that it was now or never. I'd never seen him before and we decided to meet in person for the first time. I know that it was stupid and my parents would never have let me go. So, I didn't tell them. A part of me wanted them to worry."

I reach out and put my hand around hers as she begins to sob.

31

CHARLOTTE

Dylan and I grab some lunch at a Denny's less than a mile away from James's house. We'd found the missing sister, relayed the bad news, and my stomach has been rumbling ever since bagels only a couple of hours ago.

"Feels like we should celebrate with a drink," he says.

"Or a grand slam with ten pancakes, lathered in maple syrup," I suggest.

"You know the way to a man's heart," he jokes.

"Maybe a drink when we get back?" I offer. "I don't really want to drink on the job and there's a three-hour drive ahead."

We grab a booth with a nice view of a Western motif wall and a saloon across the way.

"Have you ever been to Oatman?" I ask.

He shakes his head. "No, what's that?"

"It's this little town not too far away in Arizona. This quintessential western place and they have these burros, donkeys, wild ones coming down from the hills. It's a whole tourist attraction because you can feed them yet they're totally wild."

"What do you mean? Like, no one's in charge of them?"

"No. They just come down, visit, and go back into the hills. If you want their attention, you have to bring snacks. I always wanted to go there and it's only half an hour away from here but I don't think we can add that to the drive since we're going back with James and Madison."

"I'd like to go there, too," he says. "I love animals."

"Good. Well, maybe we can sometime."

It feels weird to make plans like this. Normally, with anyone else, I wouldn't. This is our first date after all, but after three hours in the car together, it's more like our third date or maybe even fifth.

I'm about to ask him about his family, brothers, sisters, parents, when he brings up Madison again.

"I'm really glad we found her," he says. "I thought that James was going to be a middle aged guy keeping her chained in some basement."

"Are you really such a pessimist?"

"Yes, unfortunately, I became one after a while. It's another reason I had to quit this work. You see enough carnage, death, and destruction and it warps your worldview. Doesn't it? It must."

"Yes, absolutely," I agree.

A waitress comes around and we put in our orders. She brings my Sprite and his iced tea and I take a big gulp, enjoying the cool fizz running down the back of my throat.

"That's one of the reasons I left LA. It was just too much. Had to make compromises on who I was and it was hard to do honest work within the system, at least in that department. I probably could have switched departments, but then there would have been questions and some cops would have never trusted the answers."

"You like Mesquite County?" Dylan asks.

"Yes," I say. "People are honest, hardworking. It's got a shortage of deputies though, which isn't great, but that's what happens when it's such a big area. Outside of Palm Valley, it's really rural as you know, lots of wide open desert. I like that. It's not so claustrophobic like LA was at the end."

"Oh, yeah?"

"I know I live in a quintessential suburban neighborhood right now, which I also like. A pool, wall-to-wall carpet, high ceilings, but I can see myself getting a place on a couple of acres with animals."

"Kind of like the place the Dillards have?"

"Yes. Outside the grisly murders, it looked pretty nice."

"You want to build a house yourself?" he asks.

"I don't know about that. I'm not real handy."

There are certain people that you connect with and things feel like they make sense. We're supposed to be at the diner for maybe an hour at the most but neither of us seems to want to leave. We just want to talk, lose ourselves in each other's words.

Dylan tells me about his siblings, two brothers and a sister. At first, he doesn't delve deep, briefly mentioning that one of them has issues with mental illness and drug abuse. I don't push. I give him space to tell me what he is open to sharing.

"I don't know exactly where he is," Dylan says.

When he stirs his coffee, his spoon hits the sides of the cup and makes a loud dinging sound.

"What do you mean?" I ask.

"No one in the family has had contact with him for maybe over two years. The last I heard was that he was riding trains."

"What do you mean by that?" I ask. "I thought that was just something they did back in the '50s."

"Yes, but it's still around as a practice if you can believe it. I looked into it somewhat. I interviewed a number of his friends. They're hard to find, as you can imagine. Traveling the country on trains with no documentation, hiding out from the authorities, but I managed to get in contact with a few. Two years ago in May was the last time that any of them heard anything."

"I'm really sorry," I say. "Did you put in a missing person's report?"

"Yes, of course. He was spotted in a number of states. A single man in his late thirties, with a history of drug addiction and mental illness is not exactly top priority. Plus, most people I spoke to naturally assumed that he's out on his own doing what he wants, which is something that I would have thought as well as a law enforcement officer."

"But you don't agree?" I ask.

"I do and I don't, but I still worry. We were a close-knit family. We had our problems but nothing major. My parents are together. We always met up for holidays and birthdays."

"I hope he's okay," I say.

"Hey, sorry about going on about my brother. I didn't realize that I was talking so much."

The server drops off the check. I reach for it but he takes it from me.

"Please," I say.

"Come on. It's a date, right?"

"So what? We split the bills for dates now."

"I'm not going to let you pay," Dylan says.

"Okay. Let's do 50/50. How about that?" I insist.

"Are you really trying not to make this a date?" He looks hurt.

"No, I just don't want there to be any expectations."

He finally caves after a little bit of arguing and I smile at him.

"Look, I don't want to insult you or anything but I just don't know whether I want to make this anything official," I say. "Yes, it is a date. Just not one that you can pay for quite yet."

He reaches his hand across the table, takes my hand in his, and our fingers intertwine.

"I like you, Charlotte," he says after a moment. "I like you a lot."

"I like you, too." I nod.

Then, without any prompting whatsoever, I reach over the table. I sit up in the booth, lean on the side, and reach up to kiss him. Our lips touch slightly. For a moment, he's taken aback, but then just like that, it all changes.

He kisses me back. My mouth opens slightly and our kiss becomes more passionate. We walk out of the diner holding hands and I lean slightly on him. In the parking lot, he spins me around and kisses me again, burying his fingers in my hair and tugging slightly, sending shivers up my spine.

I kiss him back. Our mouths search for meaning within one another and finding it, despite all odds. His lips are soft and yet his mouth is hard and determined at the same time. I can feel his passion for me bubbling beneath the surface.

Dylan kisses me again and again, and I kiss him back, wrapping my arms around his shoulders, pressing myself tightly against him. As a tumble weed drifts across the street under the bright blue sky of this desert town, I feel like my life suddenly makes sense.

This makes sense.

32

CHARLOTTE

On the drive back home, Dylan and I hold hands and he occasionally gives me a peck on the back of my wrist. We talk about music, which I'm not that huge a fan of but he is obsessed with. He loves classical, hip-hop, progressive rock. Almost anything and everything.

He talks extensively about the effect that Chopin has on him, as well as the significance of "La Isla Bonita", an old Madonna song about an island in Belize and how it's his dream to go there.

"I don't know much about Belize," I admit.

"It's a Caribbean country south of Mexico with sandy beaches and the second biggest coral reef in the world," he says. "I want to get a sailboat, a place with a dock, just move to a little cabin out there without a worry in the world."

"You mean you want to become one of those drunk expats, that starts boozing before noon and just keeps the party going all day?"

"Maybe." He smiles. "You've got to have a good time, right? No. Just kidding. I'll take my piano, World of Warcraft games, the series of *The Witcher* books."

"Just retire and be the nerd that you really are." I laugh.

"Yes, I guess so. So, would that be so bad?"

"No, no, it wouldn't," I admit. "I'm glad that you have so many things that you're interested in. I wish I could be more like that actually."

"Why is that?"

"Just jealous of people with hobbies and interests outside of work. The hours were really gruesome and long as a deputy. It's a little better now but still hard."

"It's not hard to have a hobby," he admits. "I just watch games on YouTube, play piano. That's about it. Been getting into building Legos, too."

"What do you like to read?" I ask.

"Fantasy, mainly, *Game of Thrones*, *The Witcher*. That's my favorite, but I do like *Star Wars* as well."

"That's great." I nod. "I've always been a big mystery thriller reader myself. Some of the latest Stephen King novels really got to me and then there's Gillian Flynn, Karin Slaughter, you know the usual suspects."

He looks at me blankly.

"They're really popular," I explain. "I like others as well. Patricia Highsmith, Raymond Chandler, different short story writers. I guess it's from when I took a few literature courses in college and they really opened up my mind about everything."

"Well, that's a hobby, reading, right? There are people that read like a book a day, a couple a week, especially when they retire."

"Yes." I nod. "I have a long way until then, but I do sometimes think that I should do more with my life than just this."

"It's not rewarding enough finding killers, bringing people to justice?"

"No, it is. It's just, I need to unlock myself, unplug."

"Well, in that case, you should read romance."

I laugh.

"I do actually. I read a lot of different books, always going back and forth to the library, picking up EBooks on my Kindle, too," I admit.

"That's great," he says.

"Okay, I'm going to tell you something that I haven't told anyone before," I say. "You ready?"

He nods.

"This part's true. I haven't shared this with anyone. It's been a secret of mine and maybe one that I should keep, but I feel like it's going to be a litmus test as well. I've been trying my hand at writing short stories."

"Really?"

"Worked about halfway through an outline for a novel."

"Oh my God, that's awesome."

Now, it's my turn to be taken aback.

"I'm a little bit surprised by your reaction." I laugh.

"Why is that?"

"I don't know. I just thought that you would make fun of me or something."

"For what? For wanting to write a novel? Isn't that the ultimate dream?"

"Not sure," I say. "I wasn't sure if I could--"

I begin a few sentences without finishing them, uncertain as to how to proceed.

"I have a couple of short stories, mysteries. three thousand, five thousand words, been working on them on my breaks and when I have the mental space to do so."

"And?" he asks.

"And it's been great. I mean, it's been exhilarating. It's like doing something you've always imagined doing and just feeling a sense of accomplishment. But the novel, I'm a little stuck on. I've read a lot of how-to books and decided that outlining is probably the best way to go but now I'm stuck on the outline."

"Well, two-thirds through the novel, you're reaching the climax, you have to figure out how to complete the story, tie up all the loose ends, right?"

I nod.

"Yes. It's easier to say than to do," I admit.

"I bet," Dylan agrees.

I pass a big delivery truck on my left and the road opens up to me completely again.

"Do you want to talk about it?" he asks. "I read mainly fantasy, but I can probably help you with some story structure or work out something in case you're stuck on a plot point. I love stories. Video games have a lot of possible outcomes as you know."

"No, not really," I admit. "I've never really played much."

"Oh, man. My college years were dominated by *Dark Age of Camelot*," he says. "I barely even made it to class. Everybody on my floor played all at once and just really built up a whole camaraderie."

"Wow, what a nerd," I joke.

"Eh, as nerdy as you imagine someone who majored in classics would be."

"What do you mean?" I ask.

"I studied Latin and Greek, a lot of Roman history, actually got into a PhD program at UCLA and was going to pursue that before I went to the police academy."

"That was quite a change of fortune," I say.

"Yes, I had some issues in my personal life at that time with my family, my brother. Right after I graduated, that was the first time he really started doing drugs, disappeared for a while. I had to look for him. My family hired a private investigator and we worked with the police. I discovered this world outside of myself. I figured, why not? It was a nice change and I liked it for a while. The camaraderie of the department, the working together, that kind of thing but things got complicated, as you know."

"Your brother disappeared a lot?"

"That was the first incident," he says. "Then, he got it together, went to medical school, and things were good for a bit. Then, in medical school, he had another episode or maybe he just fell off the wagon. I won't know for sure until we find him again. It's just all been so complicated."

"How are your parents holding up? What do they do exactly?"

"Well, they're retired now," he says. "But my father was a journalist for years. Worked for a variety of magazines and newspapers. He freelanced for a while and then wrote a couple of nonfiction books about presidents. That's when he went to DC for a year or so to do research in the archives."

"Oh, wow," I say.

"He wrote three books one on Kennedy, one on Nixon, and one on Reagan. Big exposés. He's very interested in that time period."

I nod. "Wait a second. Are you saying that you're related to Deacon M. Ferreira?"

He nods and gives me a wink. I pull my hand away from him in disbelief.

"I saw him interviewed on all of these documentaries on Netflix and PBS."

"Yes, he does a lot of interviews, gives his perspective. Subject matter expert is what they call him officially."

"Wow. That's just so impressive," I say. "Has he ever written fiction before?"

"Yes, if you can believe it, he actually used to write horror."

"Are you serious?"

"He used to write horror, detective fiction, and westerns for a variety of different magazines. That's how he paid the bills. He also wrote a number of pulp novels under various names in the '80s and early '90s. He was kind of a mid-list writer. He was also a writer for hire about different IPs."

"What does that mean?" I ask.

"Well, like *Star Trek*. He wrote a number of books for them. A company owns the rights to a world like *Star Trek* or *Star Wars* and the publisher will hire out writers who have a good knowledge base or experience writing that kind of thing to write the stories that are published within that world. That's what my dad did to pay the bills in addition to the journalism work, articles, nonfiction. He was a grind writer. He put out, tried to write four thousand words a day, five days a week. You know, sometimes it's around two thousand and other days it's seven or ten. Not all his works got published, but many did."

"It's almost as if it's a job," I joke.

"Precisely. That's what he would always say. The only way to get better is to write all the time."

Dylan pauses for a moment.

"What is it?" I ask.

"Dad wrote a lot for years and then my brother's issues started and it really broke my dad. My brother started doing drugs, started disappearing a few nights here and there a week, then longer. This time period has been the longest. Every minute that goes by, every day, I can sense that my dad is just losing hope. He tried to reach out to the cops, detectives, private investigators, anyone and everyone, and we still have nothing. Then he tried to distract himself by working on another book."

"What's it about?" I ask.

"The Kennedy assassination. Trying to write it in such a way that it's something that's more understandable and less dense, more creative. More like a mystery thriller but it's creative nonfiction."

"Didn't he write a book about Kennedy already?"

"Yes, but that was about the family, his life, his presidency, that kind of thing. The assassination was just a small part of it. This was going to be about the forces that led to his murder, including things like poor security, the choice of convertible, that kind of thing. Of course, Oswald being a communist, an outsider, and the investigations of people like that, at that time, what it meant, how many innocent people were targeted, how many probably should have been investigated even further. I think that's what he told me the last time we spoke."

"That sounds really great. Interesting," I admit.

"Yes, just not sure if he's ever going to finish it. He started this book before my brother went missing."

"So, he has writer's block?" I ask.

"Yes, he's a man who never believed in that. Never, ever. Said that you have to just work through it. It just means that you are lazy, distracted, but now he's experiencing it. Now, he can't work. He's drinking a lot more than he should," Dylan says.

"I'm so sorry."

"I have to find out what happened to John even if that means finding out that he's dead. I think any type of closure will be better than nothing."

"I agree," I say.

We don't speak for a few minutes as we pull into the city of Palm Valley. He'd left his car in front of my house. I head straight there.

Just before I turn onto my street, my phone rings. It's Madison. She and James have been driving behind us, not tandem exactly, keeping a good distance. When she calls, she tells me that she's headed straight to her grandmother's place, instead of the precinct.

"Sorry, I changed my mind. I'd rather just see them and hug them and show them I'm okay and that they can at least stop worrying about me."

"Yes, of course," I say.

"I'll be in touch later and we can make plans for official statements from everyone. Thanks."

When she hangs up, Dylan and I are alone again. When I get out of the car and start to walk slowly toward his, he pulls me close to him and kisses me. I kiss him back. After a moment, I bury my head in his chest and we hold one another.

"I want to help you find your brother," I say.

"I want to help you find your friend," he promises back.

33

CHARLOTTE

The following day, I turn my attention to the Dillards' case first thing in the morning and meet with the crime scene technicians to go over all of the business records that were found on the Dillards' computers.

The regular guy that does the laptops is out on vacation and the new one shakes my hand introduces himself as Tracy Hollis. He's an overweight man with intense eyes and stickers of *Star Wars* all over his personal laptop. When I walk in, I overhear part of his conversation on his phone about going to the new attraction at Disneyland called *Rise of the Resistance*.

"Dude, it's epic. It way exceeded my expectations. It was a whole immersive experience."

"Sorry about that," I say after he hangs up. "Didn't mean to interrupt."

"No worries. It's just, I just went this past weekend and it was amazing. It's totally trackless, dark," he tells me. "There's a good walkthrough portion, motion simulator, and a drop ride system, so it really puts you in the middle of the altercation between the Resistance and the First Order. It's almost twenty minutes long, so the whole experience is well worth the wait."

We chat a little bit about that.

"Listen, I don't know if you know this, but Madison Dillard, the older girl who went missing, I found her yesterday in Needles. She went out to meet a guy she met online. Long story short, she's perfectly fine. She was just not in touch with her family."

"Wow, that's crazy."

"Were you able to look through their records and find anything?"

"Yes, I went through a lot of the records. They worked; they had books on a lot of businesses in town."

"Anything suspicious? Anything jump out at you?"

"Well, I have some more folders to go through, but I did find something interesting."

He brings up two folders on his laptop.

"What's this?" I ask.

"There are two sets of books for the same company."

"Huh?" I tilt my head to one side. "Are you serious?"

Tracy nods his head. "One is a real set of books with their real accounts. Their real profit/loss statements, and the other is the inflated one. The fake one."

"What does that mean?" I ask. "So were they just lying on their taxes or something? Not reporting all their income?"

"That's what I thought at first, except for when you see this folder right here, I digitized it myself. In reality, it exists only in paperwork that we found in their home office."

I look at the big ledger book, open it up, and scroll through a couple of pages. He leads me about ten pages in and points to the bottom of the page, two million one hundred fifty-seven thousand six hundred eighty-nine dollars and sixty-seven cents.

"Two million?" I ask.

"Yes, and guess what? The online version of this book, the one that was on their computer, you know what the income it showed was?"

I shake my head. "No."

Fifty-seven thousand, rounding up."

"Fifty-seven grand? So what happened to the rest of the money?"

"Well, they're not reporting it."

"Wow, and who does this belong to?"

"Metcalf Associates," Tracy says. "I looked them up."

He shows me the Google search. The office is two miles away, and according to the registry, they're a bookkeeping service.

"Don't the Dillards do bookkeeping, too?"

"No, they're accountants. Metcalf Associates are bookkeepers," Tracy says. "Bookkeeping is basically a company that keeps track of the books for someone, and then the accounting firm is the one that actually files the taxes."

"So, what does this mean?"

"I don't know. I have no idea why they only have fifty-seven thousand dollars in their online account, and over two million in their paper ledger, but it looks like some sort of money laundering situation or tax fraud."

"Money laundering would mean they would inflate the numbers," I say, thinking out loud. "They're trying to clean money, so, like a drug dealer who has one hundred thousand dollars in cash from selling drugs would run that through some company to try to have a clean eighty thousand dollars or so after costs go to his pocket."

"Exactly," Tracy says.

"So this is something else."

"Yes, this is tax fraud, but more than that, they may not have gotten around to laundering yet. Perhaps they're keeping the real books to keep track of what's going on and that's why they're keeping it on paper, but something's very shady with these Metcalf Associates. That's where I would start."

"Thanks for everything." I smile and he shakes his head.

THIS HAS to be handled very carefully and, in fact, I have to run this by the lieutenant first. They're a bookkeeping firm who have done something very serious and they don't want anyone to know about this. The kind of questions that I need to ask have to be very precise and specific in order to catch them at anything.

Otherwise, I risk having them shut down. Besides the money, how is this related to the Dillards' murder anyway?

Dylan and I meet up for lunch and I catch him up on what I've found out.

Over a Caesar salad and a pasta bowl, we sit outside in the park, under the sun watching the ducks quack, walk lopsided, and jump into the water.

"I love that the station's here," he says. "It's so nice to just get out and enjoy this beautiful park."

"Yes, it's great." I nod.

I take a few bites, and as I chew, I ask him for any advice that he can offer.

He shrugs. "You have to be careful. You've got to make sure that you don't spook them, or if you do, then I guess put a tail on them to see if they go and report to anyone."

"Yes, that's what I was thinking, too. It's probably best to bring up the fraud and the Dillards at the same time. They'll deny it, of course, but maybe I can just follow them discretely or perhaps we can even get a warrant for the phones."

"Yes, it might be enough," he says. "That is a lot of fraud in those two sets of books."

"Okay, I'll talk to the lieutenant and the assistant DA. Let's see if I can get a warrant, that would be a godsend. Probably best if we can make that happen before the official conversation."

"Hey, listen, I have some other news as well."

"Oh, yes?"

"Yes. I did some more research about your friend Kelsey."

"Oh, I haven't even had time to look into that," I admit.

"But I did. There were a number of articles written about it. Not any huge publications, but there was one long story that caught my attention."

"What were you able to find?" I ask.

"The cops were pretty stumped. They figured that Kelsey went missing from a friend's house or perhaps leaving home to go to a friend's house. They know nothing about the concert you told me about or anything like that or the motel room you guys got."

"Yes, no one does. We kept that secret really well."

"I just can't believe that those cops let you lie like that."

"They didn't investigate whatsoever. If they had just talked to one of our parents and not just taken what we said at face value, I'm sure that one of us would've cracked. They didn't corroborate the stories and I have no idea why. Maybe they didn't want this kind of story in the books. Maybe they figured she wanted to run away. Who knows?"

"Her parents did move back to Seattle. I have their address and their phone number if you want to talk to them. I also have the name of the detective on the cold case that I'm sure would appreciate all the new information that you can offer. They found some bodies of girls that fit her description, ran some DNA tests and they were not a match. There were at least three different cases of human remains that were found in the Long Beach area that fit her description."

"That's something," I say. "Either that or she was taken somewhere else and the remains are just sitting in some filing cabinet under Jane Doe number whatever."

"Yes, that's also a possibility," Dylan says. "But this is something, right?"

"Of course," I agree. "It's big. I really appreciate you doing this for me."

"There's something else," he says as I scrape off the last of my salad drenched in dressing from the bottom of the bowl. I pop a soggy crouton in my mouth and chew with my mouth closed waiting for him to continue.

"There was a girl who came forward in one of these articles who said that she was Kelsey Hall."

"What?" I ask.

"Yes, it was a side note by a journalist out of Montana. He'd investigated a few different cases of mysterious disappearances and somehow stumbled upon this one. I think his mother lived in Long Beach and that's what interested him."

"What are you trying to say?" I ask.

"What I'm trying to say is that this is the article that I found. It's quite long, almost five thousand words, but here is the excerpt about Kelsey Hall."

He gives me the phone and zooms in.

"There are three paragraphs, I want you to read them."

I skim through the words trying to make sense of them. It's written in first person and the writer mentions how he received a call from a woman named Kelsey Hall who described herself as someone who fit the description of my friend.

She said that she'd gone to a concert with her friends, got lost, walked out looking for them, and then had a cute guy offer her a ride to a motel that they had booked. She doesn't remember anything after that and it took her ten years to even remember that her name was Kelsey Hall. The writer got in touch with her, but when he got her DNA, he found out that it did not match her parents'. They had refused to believe that this girl was Kelsey and didn't even want to meet her.

"Wait, what?" I ask, suddenly out of breath like someone had punched me in the gut.

"This is Kelsey," I say, pointing to Dylan's phone. "This is the story. This is what happened."

"I know, but what about the DNA? What about her parents?"

"I don't know," I say. "Maybe there was a mistake in the lab. Why didn't they want to meet her?"

"They just refused. I don't know if it was both of them or one of them or what happened exactly."

"We have to talk to this writer," I say. "This is so important."

"I agree."

I put the phone down on my lap holding it tightly in between my fingers finding it hard to believe what I have just read.

"It doesn't make any sense," I whisper.

"Kelsey Hall is a popular name. It's not so unusual."

"It was at the time," I say. "But yes, it's possible that there are more girls who fit the description who had that name."

"What about how she went missing and the motel?"

"That's the problem. The motel story didn't match the official record about how she went missing, but it matches what *you* said."

"It's her," I say. "It has to be. She's alive. The story's more than ten years old. She survived what happened, but where is she now?"

"I hope so, but she may not be. I want you to prepare yourself for that possibility, okay? I know this is a big breakthrough, but what if it's not her? What if it's not as significant as we think?"

"We have to get in touch. Will you do it for me while I work on this Dillard case?"

"Yes, I will. Do you want me to contact her parents?"

"No, not yet. I want you to find the writer first. Maybe he still has her information, but why wouldn't the DNA match?" I ask.

Dylan reaches over and gives me a squeeze on the hand.

"There are so many things that don't make sense. I'm sorry about that, but we'll get to the bottom of this, okay?"

I nod, reaching over and put my head on his shoulder. He kisses my hair.

"What if she's okay? What if, after all this time, she's not dead?"

"It's definitely a possibility," Dylan says, giving me another squeeze. I look up into his eyes and he kisses me on the mouth, and for a moment, the world falls away.

"Charlotte Pierce. Hey, Pierce!" someone yells behind me. "Lieutenant wants to see you."

It's a deputy who's only been here for two years. He has a casual way of addressing his superiors, but at this moment, I don't care. I take a deep breath.

"It's going to be okay," Dylan says. "It's going to work out."

He has no way of knowing that, but his promise makes me feel good at the moment, nevertheless.

"I've got to go," I say. "Call me tonight. Let me know if you have time to contact him and figure out what's going on."

"I will for sure," Dylan says.

34

CHARLOTTE

I'm feeling rather apprehensive going to Lieutenant Soderman's office, knowing full well that the assistant District Attorney Marilyn Donaldson is going to be there demanding answers that I can't quite give.

I like to pretend that she doesn't intimidate me, but she does. She's good at her job, honest, incorruptible, the kind of person that makes you feel like you're not doing enough, mainly because she outworks everyone at the office.

Her predecessor was fired and later prosecuted for taking bribes. Marilyn was hired with the understanding that she would be the complete opposite. She has definitely lived up to her reputation but it took a great amount of sweat equity.

Marilyn is short with reddish-blonde hair, a slim frame, and wide set eyes. Her lashes are thick with mascara, but her makeup is appropriate, giving her beauty without bringing too much attention to herself. She's dressed in a button-down shirt and gray slacks.

When I walk in and sit down in front of the lieutenant, I lean back against her jacket on my chair. I apologize briefly, but she waves her hand, nervously tapping her deep purple nails on the table.

I catch them up on the case quickly focusing on the success of finding the missing person and how happy the family is to be reunited with Madison.

"That's really great news," Marilyn says in such a way that it doesn't feel like it at all.

The lieutenant sucks down his big gulp, making a loud quenching sound that makes both Marilyn and me very uncomfortable. I wait for her to say something, but she doesn't and neither do I. We just wait for the unpleasantness to pass.

"It's a relief but, of course, I wish that you hadn't had to go there in person," the lieutenant says. "I mean, we did waste a day on this."

"Yes, I agree, but I had no idea if Madison would actually be there. I was just going to go see this guy she had met online, hoping to keep the element of surprise on my side. I didn't want the Needles Police Department to send some deputy with no experience to ruin it just in case he had killed her and stashed her body."

"Yes, of course." Marilyn nods, crossing her arms.

"The thing is that I need your help," I continue. "I need a search warrant, a tap on their phones."

"Why?"

"The Dillards had two sets of Metcalf Associates books. I want to see what happens after we have a little chat about that."

"You think they would actually admit that?" Marilyn asks.

"No, probably not. But they might make some calls afterward. They might try to cover their tracks. It's best to have a tail on them afterward as well, but first I need some insight into their communication."

"Well, first of all, you're not going to do any of that by yourself," Lieutenant Soderman says sternly.

He slams the drink down, wiping the condensation on his pants. The half-eaten sandwich from Subway is still laying open on his desk, part of it bitten into and mauled and the other kept intact.

"I want you and Will to do this together," he says. "I think we can do something about that search warrant, right, Marilyn?"

Marilyn looks up at the ceiling where a fan moves the air around slowly doing little to cool the room off.

"The double books and the brutality of the murder with the missing teeth is a lot of evidence. I'm going to run it past my boss, but I think I can make a case to go to the judge. Of course, it's up to their discretion, as you know. I'll try to run this past someone who might be the most amenable, but that's all I can promise."

"How long will it take?" I ask.

"I'll have to write up this report. I don't know, but I'll be in touch. Hopefully, later tonight if I can swing it, maybe tomorrow."

"Okay."

"In the meantime, you and Will work on the interrogation and I want to hear about your approach," the lieutenant instructs.

"I figure that the best way would be to just pretend that we don't know what's going on, that we need their help," I say. "I'll keep the part about the double books a secret for a while and maybe they'll slip up and say something before then."

"Let's hope," the lieutenant says. "Get in touch with them. Keep me updated on the progress."

"How long will it take?" I ask.

"A little bit. Once we get the warrant, we'll have to work with the phone companies. It depends on who they do business with," the lieutenant says.

I spend the rest of the day doing paperwork, filling out reports, and documenting the details of my trip to Needles. Most people don't like this part of the job. It's not action-packed. The reports have to be filled out in a very specific way, but I like it. It's mind-numbing, precise, and pretty easy if you follow the rules. I like the banality of it all. It relaxes me in a way and allows me to zone out. I finish the reports much earlier than I thought that I would.

Then I get a call from Marilyn with some bad news.

"I can't get the warrant," she says with exasperation in her voice.

"The judge just won't do it. He says that it's not enough of a connection. We have no idea if the Metcalfs had anything to do with this and we would be infringing on their rights," she says sarcastically. "Of course, if we had any idea about them actually being involved in the murders, then I wouldn't need a warrant to tap their phones. I would have a warrant for their arrest."

"I guess it was a long shot," I say.

"No, it wasn't. This judge doesn't like to take chances and no one else was available. He's very worried about his decisions being overturned."

I nod despite the fact that we're on the phone and she can't see me.

I know that she did her best in trying to get a warrant and I'm not sure what else I can do.

"I want you and Will to follow the Metcalfs after you speak to them, follow them and see where they go and what they do. There's a good chance that they're going to avoid the telephone anyway. If it's something serious, they might go talk to them in person, and you don't need a warrant to trail them to see who they're talking to."

Marilyn is the type of person who has a tendency to talk a lot when she gets nervous and she starts to make her case over and over again.

The truth is that this is a big blow. The tapping of the phones would've been great and though the Metcalfs could be master criminals who would go out of their way to avoid the telephone, I doubt that.

In reality, almost anyone in their situation would pick up the phone and call whoever they had a problem with. Having access to that information would go a long way in making this case but, until I get more evidence, it's out of my hands.

"Will and I are going to go there first thing tomorrow morning when the office opens."

"Again, I'm sorry," Marilyn says. "Please, keep in touch."

35

CHARLOTTE

That evening on the way home I get a text from Dylan that he has some news to share with me, but he wants to do it in person.

"Sure. Come on over. We can get takeout," I offer.

When I get home that evening, he's standing in front of me with two bags of Indian food and a smile.

"Wow, this is great," I say. "This is exactly what I need after the day I've had."

When we get inside, he puts the bags on the island in the kitchen and mentions how nice my house is. It's probably a little bit too big for one person, but I really like it and, at this point, I've grown into it.

"At this rate, you are going to get sick of me soon," I joke. "We spent all that time together yesterday, lunch and dinner. I'm afraid that in a few more dates, we might go through a whole relationship."

He looks at me, his lips turned downward, like my words have really hurt him.

"I really doubt it," Dylan says. "The more time I spend with you, the more time I *want* to spend with you."

"Yes, of course." I wave my hand. "I was just joking."

"You have a beautiful home," he says, walking around the foyer, looking at the asymmetrical modernist mirror that I had put up myself with great difficulty.

I bought it on a whim. It cost and weighs too much, but it's a perfect fit.

The rug is aged, but in that production manner kind of way where it came out of the factory. The hues of orange and magenta and the little bit of blue and teal really shine in the sunlight streaming in through the tall glass sliding door that spans the entire far wall of the house, looking out onto the pool.

"When I was growing up, I didn't think that I could ever live in a house like this," I say. "When I was a kid, I had this negative perception of the suburbs. Thought they were stifling people with their cookie-cutter appearance. I dreamed of living in some big city, thought that it would make me important. But after a decade in LA with eighteen dollar drinks and drunks peeing on the stoops of my tiny apartments, I got sick of it."

"I know exactly what you mean," he agrees. "It just didn't seem worth it. I mean, I could buy a bottle of wine from Trader Joe's for two dollars, and a glass would cost like twelve dollars at a nearby restaurant. It wasn't just that. I didn't realize just how much I would enjoy having a backyard, a pool, and a garage for my car and a little gym."

"Maybe we're just getting older or something, but it just feels nice." I laugh. "Plus none of the neighbors make any noise, or if they do they're far enough away that it doesn't even matter."

"Your house is beautiful," he says. "It's kind of what drew me to Palm Valley, too. I traded in my studio apartment for a three-bedroom house so that's something, and the weather's much better."

"Yes. I wish that people wouldn't discover the secrets of this place and come streaming in but, at the same time, I want to run and yell from the rooftops about how great and beautiful it is. Look at that mountain," I say, taking him to the window.

He opens the sliding door and we walk out onto the big grassy patch near the pool. From here, you can stand and see the surrounding mountains still covered in snow even though it's seventy-eight degrees down here on the valley floor.

Dylan intertwines his hands with mine and pulls me closer, giving me a kiss. I kiss him back.

"You want to show me the rest of your house?" he asks.

I tilt my head, looking at him mischievously. He gives me a wink.

"Think it might be a little too early to see the bedroom," I say.

"Hey, I promise I'll be a gentleman."

"I'm not sure if that's what I want," I joke. He smiles and I laugh and it feels like the most natural thing in the world.

We walk through the rest of the house. He tests out my worn sectional, which is comfortable, but not exactly aesthetically pleasing. I show him the guest room with the queen-size bed and the room that I've converted into my office.

"I've never shown this place to anyone," I say right before I open the door. "Not even my friends, so don't laugh."

"Of course not."

"It's just like a place of inspiration, okay?"

"Listen, I'm here for you. I understand hobbies and passion, don't worry. I have a three bedroom because one room is taken up by my Lego projects."

I open the door and the first thing we see is a large oak growing outside of the window. The room looks to the outside while the rest of the house faces inward toward the backyard.

When the gardeners are here, it's quite busy, but luckily that's just on Tuesdays and I'm mostly at work during that time.

One side of the room is covered in white bookshelves reaching all the way almost to the top of the ceiling. They're not built-ins, but they're made to look like that. On the other side, I have a standing desk and a gaming chair.

The desk has little wheels on the bottom and it's usually in front of the bookcase. But for the last couple of days, I've moved it over to the window so I can have a nice view. The walls of the office are lined with posters of famous writers at work next to their desks. I looked them up online and printed and framed the pictures.

There is Stephen King reclining in his messy office with his feet on the table and his typewriter nearby in black and white, and there's Danielle Steel in front of her bright colored desk made from the covers of her bestselling books. Mark Twain is in the corner, standing regal and full of wit and no-nonsense as well as Ray Bradbury. Flannery O'Connor is feeding chickens outside of her home. I couldn't find one of her in front of a typewriter, but this was good enough. I like it for its pastoral quality.

"Oh my God, my father's going to love you," Dylan says, shaking his head.

"Flannery O'Connor is probably one of his favorites. He always talks about how little credit Danielle Steel is given despite her giant popularity, especially in the literary circles."

"I'd like to meet him sometime," I say, even though personally I feel incredibly intimidated.

"At first, I wasn't sure what to do with this room. But I figured why not. No one comes in here. No one would even have to know if I did anything with it, so I just went for it one day. Got the pictures first and it was just really inspiring to see these writers at work. Can you think that of people you've never met as friends based on the words they write? That's how I felt and I just wanted them to surround me and give me inspiration. Over here, I have writers who are more indie."

"What does that mean?" Dylan asks.

"Independently published. They write a lot, publish a lot, but outside the traditional New York system. It's really exciting the kinds of things that these people publish. I've joined a few Facebook groups and the fact that they can just make a living doing this, is absolutely amazing. I can't imagine that that could be me, but I like to try it."

"You could totally do it," Dylan says, taking my hand. "I mean, you already have short stories. You have this outline of a novel. Why not? You said so yourself, these people over here on this wall are doing it. Willow Rose, Blake Pierce, Wayne Stinnett, Craig Martelle. If they're doing it so can you. Right?"

"Yes, I guess so."

I doubt that he will ever know the extent to which his support fuels me and gives me this air and the ability to fly. People make fun of the concept of mindset like it's something fake, but belief in oneself and the sheer knowledge that you can do this, overcome any obstacle no matter what, is one of the most important things in life.

I did that when I applied to USC, which seemed to be so out of the realm of possibility as a place that would accept me. I did that when I went to the police academy.

With writing, it would be the same way. Whatever my path would be I just had to believe in it enough and take the steps to make those dreams come true.

Small steps. The short story is first. Then finishing the outline, then the first chapter and so on.

A large goal is a result of results from a million little goals.

I tell myself this because it's easy to forget. It's easy to just let this go and not work on something when it's hard, when you're exhausted, and you haven't had much sleep, but that's one of the most important things.

"Thank you," I say to Dylan, looking straight into his eyes. "It's hard to explain, but you have this dream in your mind and you take steps to complete it, but it's nice to have someone else in your corner. It makes me feel like it's actually doable, like you believe in me."

"Always," he says.

"You haven't even read what I've written," I joke.

"What if you were to read something in fantasy or sci-fi?" Dylan asks. "You're not the primary demographic. What does it matter whether you like it or not? It doesn't. What matters is that there are readers out there that will, and you're writing for *them.* But mostly you're writing for you, right? This is *your* story. This is how you want to tell it. You want to sell it, but you're going to sell it to those readers."

"What about your father?" I ask. "You can't tell him I'm a writer."

"I won't, but I'm sure you will yourself. Don't worry about my father. He knows exactly where you're coming from. He's somebody who worked really hard to get where he is and he actually gives back a lot. He doesn't believe in pushing people down. He's not that kind of writer."

"You mean he's not an ass?" I joke.

"He is in some things, but not this." Dylan smiles.

"I think our food is getting cold." I suddenly remember. "Let's go back to the kitchen and you can tell me what you found out about Kelsey."

36

CHARLOTTE

Over palak paneer and mushroom korma, Dylan fills me in on the Zoom call that we're about to have in less than an hour.

He got in touch with Jonathan Chabon, the journalist who now lives in Montana, who wrote that article about Kelsey Hall.

"Does he have any idea that we're talking about the same person?" I ask.

"I haven't talked to him much but I wanted to question him with you on the Zoom call and he was very willing to talk."

"He's pretty certain that it is her but the DNA didn't match," I say. "How could that be?"

"I don't know and he doesn't either but once I told him who you were, and what happened, he was very interested."

"What do you mean, what happened? You told him *my* story?" I gasp.

"No, I didn't go that far. I didn't share any details because I wanted to hear what he had to say first. Why don't we just save all of our questions until it's time for us to talk?"

"That's easier said than done. For sure."

We eat in silence the rest of the time and all I can think about is the conversation that's about to happen. We set up the laptop on my kitchen table and huddle next to each other testing out the technology a few times to make sure that the lighting and the sound are good. Dylan even looks up how to record it to make sure that none of the updates changed the process of doing so.

Right at the designated time, Jonathan appears on screen and joins our call. He is in his mid-fifties but fit with a big mop of grayish-brown hair. He's dressed in a North Face pullover and his face is tan with a few lines here and there. Even over video, it's clear that he's no stranger to staying active in the outdoors.

We introduce ourselves and when there's a slight lull in the conversation as I try to figure out where to start, Jonathan jumps right in.

"You're Kelsey's friend?" he asks. "That's what Dylan told me. Is that why you're looking for her?"

"Yes, I'm a detective and I was friends with her in middle school. We were close."

"Do you believe what the investigators are saying about how she disappeared? The manner in which she disappeared?"

I'm about to say something when Dylan interrupts.

"Jonathan, hold on a second. Before we answer your questions, can you just go through what happened and how you got in contact with her? I promise that we will tell you everything we know."

"On the record?" Jonathan asks.

"Yes. I'm not sure about being on the record right now. You can definitely take notes," Dylan says, "but this is an ongoing investigation that's going to be reopened so before anything is published, you need to double check for our permission."

"Okay, fair," Jonathan agrees.

"Now can you please tell me in greater detail what you briefly told me over the phone?"

Jonathan tilts his head, leans back in his chair, and puts his hands above his head.

Stretching his back slightly, he then leans back down and says, "Kelsey reached out to me when the police wouldn't. She lives not far away from here and she told me that she'd read some of my articles in the Montana Review, which is famous for its creative nonfiction pieces. She wanted someone thorough and trustworthy."

"What was her story?" I ask.

"She said that her name is Kelsey Hall. She said that she has no memory of what happened that night or what happened for weeks, or months, after her disappearance. She has no idea how she ended up in a brothel in Miles City in someone's two bedroom apartment with a lot of indigenous girls."

"You mean like Native American?" I ask.

He nods. "Miles City is a dusty outpost on the plains, used to be an oil town, but not anymore."

"She was working there for a while with not a great memory of who she was before, or what had happened. She was just living her daily life, hopped up on drugs that the pimps provided her and forced her to take. Then a man came in, a Marine. He saw her a couple of times and they made a connection. He asked her if she was being held there against her will and she said yes. She wanted to leave but she didn't know how and so he helped her. He came back again, parked his car nearby, and helped her climb out of the window. It was a simple escape."

"Why didn't they go to the authorities?" I ask.

"The problem was that he was an active serviceman. He's not supposed to go to brothels, have sex for money, do anything unbecoming of a Marine. He was worried that he would get dishonorably discharged and he wanted to make the military his career. She promised that she would wait to go to the cops until he was deployed. Two months later, when he was out of the country, she filed the report but didn't mention him,. She kept his name a secret because she didn't want to get him in trouble."

"Okay, and did they take it seriously?"

"Miles City PD investigated. I checked with the vice detective. He went to the apartment, but they were gone. The landlord refused to acknowledge that any illicit activities were taking place because, of course, he didn't want to get in trouble and no one else would talk. The place just moved. It's like it never even existed. She had no proof of what had happened to her there and all the girls were gone, too."

"How many girls were there?"

"Four, when she was there, one left to go work somewhere else, they rotated in and out and she was supposed to be sent away as well. The whole point is to not stay in one place too long because you do have repeat customers and they do tend to talk and make connections. After she took off, they all disappeared."

"So, what happened after?" I ask.

"She reached out to me much later because she saw something on the news."

"You mean she didn't even know her name was Kelsey Hall?" I ask.

"She had no idea. Not until she saw a picture of herself and the name. She thought her name was Maria Dorita, or so they told her. She had no ID. Nothing."

"How old was she when this happened? Does that match up with her age?"

"Yes. She worked there for a long time. She thought it had been a couple of years but in reality, we worked it out and it was a lot longer. They kept her in a fog of drugs and she still struggles. She has certain issues but she's been to rehab a few times and has been sober for a while."

I am skeptical and I know that he can sense that. That's when he reaches over and shares the screen and a picture of Kelsey pops up.

My mouth drops open.

"I have to go," Dylan says, starkly out of the blue. "There's an emergency, big fire. I'm on call today but you guys keep talking. Okay? I'll see you later."

He squeezes my hand. I nod in his direction and return my gaze back to the screen.

"It's her, isn't it?" Jonathan asks, leaning closer to the camera.

Her face fills up the screen as he goes through a slideshow. She looks exactly like I remember her. But worn out, tired, with gray skin and big bags under her eyes.

He leaves the pictures on the screen and tells me how skeptical he was at first. She told him a story. She wasn't sure that it was her but she wanted to confirm because she was so confused about everything.

"What happened?" I ask.

"Well, I interviewed her. We talked. I became convinced that it was possibly her. I saw pictures of her parents and I saw their interviews on the news and there was a striking resemblance. I reached out to the parents but they weren't sure. Apparently, they had other people try to scam them for money by using information about her. I finally asked if they would be willing to submit their DNA through the police in Washington so that we could compare it to her. They agreed. They refused to even meet with her and I had to agree that she would not be anywhere near the station when this happened."

"They really didn't think it was her?"

"No. Apparently, they had sent ten thousand dollars to someone a few years into her disappearance. This person claimed to hold her hostage and that money vanished. On another occasion, they met with someone claiming to be her. She didn't want any money but she told them that they had a grandchild that they needed to support."

"Wow, that's really messed up," I say, shaking my head. "I guess I don't fault them for thinking that she's just another faker."

"They were proven right when the DNA didn't match. They stopped talking to me after that, refused to answer any of my questions. Didn't even want to consider why the DNA wasn't a match."

"You think that something happened at the lab?" I ask.

"I'm not sure. There're a lot of possibilities."

Jonathan shows me more pictures of Kelsey now. She has long flowing hair, her nose is slim. She has fillers in her cheeks and lips and she doesn't look at all like the earlier pictures that he had shown me.

"She started a new life," he says. "She got married. She has two kids. We spoke ten years ago so she's in recovery for her alcoholism and drug addiction. Going to meetings, hasn't used in probably seven years. I don't fault her for getting a new look. When I met her, she was emaciated."

"That's probably why she looked so much like her twelve-year-old self," I say out loud.

"Yes, probably. She lives in Las Vegas and both of her kids are under eight."

"But it's not her, right? I mean, why would the DNA not match her parents?"

"There's a small likelihood something happened at the lab. I mean, by accident, because I don't see a reason why anyone would switch that out. It's not a murder case or anything like that, but maybe it's something else."

"Like what?" I ask.

He shrugs. "I'm not sure. I have no idea."

My eyes veer from the most recent picture of plastic-looking Kelsey Hall with her plump face and her overdone makeup and her healthy weight against the pictures that Jonathan showed me from when they first met.

The girl looks almost identical to the twelve-year-old that I knew. That's when I tell him the truth about that night. What really happened and how the cops were wrong and they didn't know the whole story.

"Wait a second. That's exactly what Kelsey told me," Jonathan says. "That she went to a concert and got separated from her friends. She remembered that for sure. When she walked out of the concert venue, she got picked up by a cool looking guy in a red convertible who promised to give her a ride to her motel."

"Yes, that's all true. We did get a motel room. It was a little bit away from the arena. She went back for her scarf and that's how we lost her."

"The police didn't know any of this?" Jonathan asks.

I shake my head no.

"That's why I reached out to you," I say. "I knew you had my Kelsey because you wrote the story that no one else could have known."

Neither of us says a word for a moment.

"But the DNA doesn't match," I say.

Jonathan whispers, "I know."

37

CHARLOTTE

A sound in the middle of the night startles me. It beeps the signal that one of the doors has been opened.

My heart jumps into my throat and I pop out of bed. I typically don't carry my Glock with a five inch barrel off duty and have swapped it out for my sub-compact Smith and Wesson 442 in a .38 special.

Flipping off the sound machine that I use to sleep, I listen for footsteps in the living room. I grip the revolver with my right hand and wrap my left hand's fingers around the dominant hand to stabilize it.

Leaning my back against the wall, I make my way around corners and crouch down behind the couch.

The footsteps are coming from the kitchen.

I don't want to shoot him, let alone kill him, but I'm willing to do both. Who the hell is he and why is he here?

To catch him by surprise, I flip on the dining room lights just as I see his body head in that direction. The dining room and the kitchen are separated by a doorway, but the living room has access to both.

The bright lights startle him and he jumps.

"Hey." I point the gun.

"Don't shoot, it's me. I didn't want to wake you."

I recognize his voice immediately and lower the weapon.

"What are you doing here, Dylan? Why are you breaking into my house?" I walk over to him, punching him in the shoulder.

"I didn't want to wake you, but I wanted to see you again."

"So, you were just going to sneak up on me?"

"I tried your front door, but it was locked and I was just going to leave if the sliding door was locked, too, but it was open. You should really keep it locked."

"And you should really not enter people's premises without permission. I mean, I could have shot you."

"Yes. I can see that now."

"I have an alarm that tells me if any of the doors are open and it woke me up, I guess, for good reason. But, seriously, what are you doing here?"

"We put out the fire at this big warehouse and I was thinking of driving home, but then I drove past your house and I just wanted to see you again. See how it went with that reporter."

"You want to talk about that at 2:00 a.m.?"

"No, that's just an excuse."

He smiles and dims the lights. A streak of moonlight comes through, bathing us in that cold blue light. I can see the soot from the fire on his face, dried, sweat as well. He looks handsome. His eyelashes flutter as if they were butterfly wings and I reach over and tuck a loose strand of dark lush hair behind his ear.

"You wanted to see me?" I ask.

He leans down, puts his finger underneath my chin, and tilts it slightly up toward him.

"I missed you," he whispers and kisses me on the mouth.

I kiss him back. My hands make their way up his broad shoulders and into his hair burying my fingers in his mane. He pulls me close, his fingers running up underneath my night shirt.

I'm dressed in an oversized T-shirt and a loose pair of shorts. I revel in the swiftness of his fingers as they run up my bare back, sending shivers of excitement back down.

His hands cradle my head as we kiss more and more and he pushes me against the wall. He pulls away slightly, looking deeply into my eyes, and presses his lips to my neck.

"Where's your bedroom?" he asks.

I bite my lip.

"You either tell me or I'll go find it." He grabs my hand.

He has seen the guest room and the office and he leads me down the long hallway which I had previously indicated led to my bedroom.

I have a bench at the foot of my king-size bed and he tosses me over it. I can't help but laugh but the smile quickly vanishes when he drapes my body with his.

"I should take a shower first."

The smoke in his hair and skin mixed with the saltiness of the sweat is intoxicating, manly.

"I've never had a thing for firefighters until now," I say jokingly.

"Well, you should see me in my uniform," he whispers. "Maybe next time I can put on a little show."

His hand makes its way up my shirt. I pull away slightly from his mouth and roll my tongue up and down his neck, feeling his body press harder and harder into mine. He pulls off his T-shirt and I see the perfect outline of his six-pack.

"Wow," I whisper.

"You're so beautiful," he says and kisses me again and again, pulling my shirt over the top of my head.

AFTERWARD, lying naked next to one another in a daze of ecstasy, Dylan turns toward me, propping his head up with his hand.

"Do you mind if I take a shower?" he asks.

"Of course not."

"I still can't believe that you almost shot me. This night could have gone a completely different way."

"Yes. It's a good thing I flipped on that light switch. But note to self for you, do not climb into anyone's houses in the middle of the night. You never know what's going to happen, especially if someone has a gun."

"Okay, point taken. I mean, I knew that of course but just didn't quite expect you to do that."

When Dylan walks to the shower, I admire the strength of his thighs. He's clearly no stranger to the gym.

"You work out a lot?" I ask, pulling on my T-shirt.

"Hey, don't get dressed," he says, grabbing my hand.

"It's cold in here," I lie, when really I'm just a little bit uncomfortable standing stark naked in the bathroom.

When the water is sufficiently warm, he goes inside and tugs at me.

"I'll give you a second," I protest.

A moment later, when the black stuff on his skin goes down the drain, I climb in and we make love again. I like being in his arms, feels comfortable and safe, and that's more than I've felt in a very long time.

Afterward, it's so late, it's morning again. I don't know if I'll be able to sleep and I have a long day in front of me. But I try to get a little bit of shut-eye, and so does he. When my alarm goes off in the morning, just an hour and a half later, I feel less than refreshed.

He rouses a little but I tell him to keep sleeping, that I have some work to get to before going to the station. Dylan doesn't listen. Instead, he forces himself to his feet, goes to the kitchen, and makes us a big omelet with mushrooms, spinach, cheese, and avocado.

"Okay, don't get your hopes up. I'm not a very good cook, but I do like a good breakfast, and I'm trying to make an impression," Dylan jokes.

"You're working on an hour of sleep. You need to rest," I say.

"Yes, I will once you go to work. If you don't mind of course."

"No. I'll leave you the spare key so you don't have to break and enter next time."

"Ah, funny," he says, using the spatula to point at me and give me a wide toothy smile.

Over a breakfast and tea for me, coffee for him, I catch Dylan up about what happened with the rest of my conversation with Jonathan Chabon about Kelsey. I tell him my concerns, but also my belief that it is the real Kelsey Hall that contacted him back then.

"She doesn't look the same anymore, which is completely fine of course, this was twenty years ago, but I just can't believe that the DNA isn't a match. I guess they could have made a mistake at the lab, but how are we going to prove it now? I just can't believe that her parents would go through the rest of their lives not knowing that it's her."

"Does she remember them?" Dylan asks.

"No, I don't know what happened or why she has this amnesia or whatever it's called. I have to talk to her, this person that doesn't even go by Kelsey Hall anymore. Then I'll know for sure that it's my friend."

"What if she doesn't remember you, doesn't remember anything about you?"

"That's a possibility, but I'll remember her. Her mannerisms, certain things about her have to be there, right? She wasn't a three-year-old. She was twelve. Twelve is different."

"Yes. I agree," Dylan says.

We talk about this a little more going in circles. Nothing will be resolved until I can actually meet her either on video chat or in real life. Of course, I'd prefer real life.

"So, tell me about the fire. What happened? Is it common for you to be called in like that?"

"Actually, no, not really. During fire season, yes. Fires start all over California and we get sent to wherever we are needed. Mostly down here in the south, since there are so many fires, but this warehouse fire was unusual. It belonged to some e-commerce business that was selling goods on Amazon."

"What do you mean?" I ask.

"Amazon doesn't sell anything directly. You can sign up to be an Amazon seller and buy directly from China or wherever you have manufacturing and sell that stuff on Amazon. They're kind of a clearinghouse. They have a few of their own brands and there are, of course, big names but one of the things that made that company so successful is the small business angle of it. You can just set up an account, have Amazon warehouse your stuff, and send it directly whenever people buy it. You can play the algorithm game, figure out which products are very popular, source those, set up the distribution, and make a margin."

"Was this what they were doing?" I ask.

"Yes, precisely." He nods. "This whole warehouse was set up to do that."

"You mean it was run by Amazon?"

"Well, they have their own fulfillment services, but this company, I guess, got big enough that they were selling stuff directly from their own warehouse."

"What kind of things were they selling?"

"Hard to tell. Pots, pans, some linens. I think it was like a Home Goods kind of place, but that's all I know."

"Uh-huh." I nod. "Well, does it look like it was a suspicious fire?'

"They're going to be doing an arson investigation. Just from looking at it, I would say yes, there were multiple places where the fire started and that's usually the number one sign. Of course, it could have happened spontaneously as well. That's what the arson investigator's going to do. But there's one thing that I found particularly curious that I think will be of great interest to you."

"What?" I say.

"After we put out the fire and while I was talking to some of the guys and the deputies on the scene, we found out from the paperwork in the office that partially survived that this warehouse was owned by Metcalf Associates."

"What?" I gasp.

"Yes," he says.

"You mean the bookkeeping company?"

"Yes. There were a lot of bills in their name and the warehouse was actually registered in their name."

"I wonder what that means," I whisper.

"I don't know. I guess it's up to you to find out."

"What does a bookkeeping service have to do with an e-commerce business," I wonder out loud.

WHEN I GET TO WORK, Will is already there. He has talked to the lieutenant and we're going to be going to the Metcalf's office to confront them about the double books. I fill him in on the details of the fire and the fact that the warehouse was owned and operated by them.

"After Dylan told me that this morning," I say, "I called the fire chief and the arson investigator and they confirmed that paperwork was indeed found with their names on the lease as well as operational materials and the business license."

"Wait a second," Will says, looking at me like he has an epiphany.

I wonder what I missed.

"*Dylan* told you this *morning*?" He gives me a wink. "Does that mean he slept over?"

I roll my eyes. This is not where I expected him to go.

"Yes. Well, he slept over last night. Actually, the story is much more convoluted than that but let's just put it that way."

"I have to hear this. What happened?"

We grab coffee at the little stand outside and I fill him on the details.

"You almost shot him?" Will smiles. "Are you serious?"

"Yes. That would've been not such a good outcome," I state the understatement of the century.

"Well, I'm glad you didn't."

"Yes, me, too." I laugh. "And we had a good time afterward, that's all I'm saying."

"I need more details."

"You sicko," I joke and he laughs.

"If you're happy, I'm happy. Let's just leave it at that," Will says.

38

CHARLOTTE

Will and I haven't been on a stakeout in ages, and while at first it's a little foreign, we quickly fall back into our natural groove. We joke around for a while, and then he asks me more seriously about Dylan.

"Is this a one-time thing, just a fun guy to have around or what?"

"Hey, it's only been a few dates," I say.

"Yes, but the whole sleeping over thing is new, right? Oh, wait, are you testing out the car before you buy it?"

"You have to, right?" I joke, and then I tell him about the drive over to Needles and how he surprised me.

"Well, that could have backfired massively," he says, taking a few gulps of his Coke. He usually doesn't drink any soda except for when he's on a stakeout because it gives him something to look forward to. His words, not mine.

The thing about this part of the job is that you wait and wait, and then you wait some more. This wasn't our idea exactly, but the lieutenant is trying to buy some time and he wants us to be productive in the meantime. The assignment is to go to Metcalf Associates' office building and watch for any activity.

We have to sit here and take note of all visitors, doing the job that any camera could do. Still, here we are.

"How long do you think this is going to last?" I ask Will.

He shrugs. "I have a feeling that it's going to be until we get the warrant."

"Well, the fact that the warehouse is connected has to mean something, right?"

"I hope so but, of course, the DA has to make a whole case of it to the judge, the judge has to think about it, approve the warrant. Who knows how long that takes. It's not like they are in any hurry."

"Well, that's not true," I joke, and he takes another gulp. "You're going to be through that in a minute."

"So what?"

"If you go through the whole six pack, you'll need to use the restroom soon and then I'll have to sit here and do *our* job myself."

"You're free to go to the bathroom, too."

"Do you see one around here? It's not like we're in some busy shopping area, this is just a business park," I say, pointing to the offices all around. "We can't leave, and I don't want you going into any building."

"Okay, okay, I'll take it easy," Will promises, twiddling with the metal piece on top of the can until it pops off in his palm. He has a tendency to fidget when he's annoyed and frustrated and bored. In this situation, we're all of those things at once.

"I have to talk to you about something," Will says, tapping his hand on the steering wheel.

"Oh, what?"

"I think I'm in trouble." He licks his lips and looks out of the driver's side window at the crow jumping on top of the Mexican palm.

"What are you talking about?"

"The lieutenant found out about me seeing Erin Lowry."

"How?"

"He caught us," Will says, turning away from the window and looks directly at me.

"He saw us kissing in the movie theater."

"What did he say?"

"Nothing, that's what's so strange about the whole situation."

"When did this happen?"

"Two days ago."

I bite the inside of my cheek trying to think of what could have taken so long for the lieutenant to confront him about it.

"So, what happened exactly?" I ask.

"We were in the movie theater, we went to see *Batman*, and we were sitting in the back in one of those big recliners and started making out."

"What are you, in high school?" I ask.

He shrugs.

"You can't do that at home?"

"We've done that already, but we wanted to go out. We wanted to be like a normal couple."

"But you're not a normal couple," I say. "Erin was the primary suspect in the murder of her husband and his wife, you were the primary investigator on that case. Your relationship is very inappropriate."

"Yes, I know that, but she had nothing to do with it."

"Yes, but someone else might say that the case got dismissed against her because of *you*. Don't act like you don't realize the implications of all of this. Tell me what happened with the lieutenant."

"Well, he was there with his wife and he walked past me, we locked eyes."

"He saw you?"

"It was dark, but yes, I saw him."

"He recognized you, and he recognized her?" I ask.

"I can't be certain, but I would have. He's seen her plenty on the news and she was interviewed a few times as well."

"He saw you kissing, not just right afterward?"

"He was kind of waiting in line to go up, and he bumped into my leg slightly. That's what caused me to pull away and look up and he apologized."

"Then what?"

"Then he just walked on," Will says.

"There may be a chance that he didn't really recognize you if it was dark and the movie was going."

"Yes, that's a possibility," Will admits. "Not a good one, but I guess it's possible."

"What else could it be?" I ask.

"I have no idea, I thought he would call me into his office the next day, but he didn't. I was on pins and needles the whole time. Then the following day when he called me in, he assigned me to this case and said we're going to do a stakeout together."

"He may be waiting for a good time to talk to you," I say.

"Maybe."

"There are a number of possibilities of what he might be doing," I say. "One is that he didn't recognize you which seems highly unlikely."

"Yes, I agree."

"Two, he recognized you, but is waiting to talk."

"Waiting for what?" Will asks.

"I don't know. Maybe until this case is over, but who knows when that will be."

"But why assign me to this case if I wasn't on it already?" he asks.

"I don't know the answer to that, either."

"Any other possibilities?" Will asks.

"What if he's trying to pretend that he has no knowledge of it, plausible deniability?" I ask. "If he didn't see you there, if he didn't see you two kissing, then nothing improper happened. He didn't confront you. He didn't talk to you about it. He can easily deny it to Internal Affairs that no, he has absolutely no knowledge of it."

"Huh," Will says, sitting back in his seat. "Wow, that would be very smart but sneaky, huh?"

"Yes, I agree." I nod. "He may be trying to protect himself and you in the process."

We don't say anything for a few minutes, ruminating on what the lieutenant could and couldn't be thinking.

"I could ask him about it," I offer not in any realistic way, "but then it would bring the whole thing to the surface and I'm not sure anybody wants that. Plus at this point, he doesn't know that *you* know. Or I know."

Will points out and says, "I'm not sure if we actually want him to know, right?"

"No, I wouldn't say that."

"Plausible deniability? Should I just hope that's what's going on?"

"It's been two days. Maybe he's turning a blind eye trying to protect you, the department, the whole case."

"Okay, I hope so," Will says.

When the day begins to wear on and Will starts to complain about needing to use the bathroom, a black Camaro pulls up to Metcalf Associates, parking partly over the line of the handicapped parking spot and taking up two spots at once.

A big, tall man with a receding hairline jumps out, slamming the door shut. His phone is attached to his belt and rides on his hip as if it were a gun.

His substantial belly hangs over his belt and he's clearly agitated.

"Wait a second," Will says. "I know that guy!"

39

CHARLOTTE

"How do you know him?" I ask.

"You know him, too. Look," Will says. "It's Barr Houser."

"And who's that?" I ask.

"He is one of the biggest organized crime lords of Mesquite County. Runs drugs and women. He escaped a murder charge a couple of years back. Went all the way to trial, found not guilty, but he did it. Everyone knew it. There just wasn't enough evidence. Well, there was enough evidence, but a bunch of it didn't get included for various legal technicalities."

"What is he doing here?" I ask. "These Metcalf Associates are definitely some shady people."

Barr slams through the office door in a huff. We don't follow him inside. Instead, I zoom in on him with the telephoto lens.

The windows in the office are tinted and it's hard to see, but a few minutes later, he rushes back out to his car with someone behind him.

"Wait, that's Terry Treas," Will says.

"Who's that?"

"He's a famous, almost, pro golfer. He actually was one of the people that was going to testify against Barr until something happened. We've got to check the paperwork on the warehouse and Metcalf again. These two names have to be there."

"What if they're using pseudonyms?"

"Or registered under someone else entirely?" he suggests.

We look over at Barr and Terry Treas, who are about to get into a fight. Hands are flying all over the place and they are yelling.

Barr pulls away and gets back into his car, rolling down the window.

"You're going to pay for this, Terry!" he yells. "You have no idea who you're messing with. Go fuck yourself!"

This portion of the conversation comes in loud and clear.

"God, I wish we'd had those bugs put in," I say. "We could have gotten all of this on tape."

"No, the bugs would've only been for their phones, but this is a good time to confront Mr. Terry Treas," Will suggests. "Maybe he has something meaningful to contribute or at least tell us about his recent enemy, right? What do you think?"

Just to make sure, I call the lieutenant to fill him in on what happened.

"Any chance that the warrant is going to come in for the phones?" I ask. "Otherwise, I think we should go in right now and have that chat."

"You might as well," the lieutenant says with a tinge of disappointment in his voice. "I don't want to waste any more time. What the hell is Barr doing there?"

"Whatever he's doing anywhere," I say.

Will says, "Nothing good."

Will and I go over the conversation of how it might go. Neither of us have any good ideas about what will actually happen, but that's part of the fun.

"Let's take it easy at first," Will suggests. "Treat Terry with kid gloves. Maybe Barr made him just angry enough that he'll have something to say. If that doesn't work, we can try to scare him, pretend that we know more than we know."

"Oh, you don't think that we should just bust in there and make all sorts of threats and wait for his lawyer to get back to us?" I ask sarcastically.

Will rolls his eyes.

"Okay, but before we go in, I really have to use the bathroom."

He starts the engine and we drive to the nearest 7-Eleven, making light of the whole thing. We're both putting on a good face about not being as nervous as we really are. Those butterflies in the pit of your stomach can be a good thing. They put you on edge, make you hyper-alert and aware of your circumstances.

That's both a good thing and a bad thing.

It's easy to make a mistake and to say the wrong thing, push someone over the edge or not push enough, but Will and I have done this plenty of times.

We know how the game is played. We also work well together. Being able to communicate with your partner with a few vocal cues is important. I can sense his tension and I can sense when he is feeling the pressure. I know when he's going to build up his anger on a possible suspect and when he's going to pull back, and I think he knows the same about me.

The second time we pull up to the Metcalf Associates office, we park right out front for everyone to see. In fact, I wish we had our county-issued vehicle with lights for full intimidation, but this will work, too.

The office is pretty nondescript. The building is one story high and the bell on the glass door makes a loud dinging sound when we walk in. This office space is a little bit nicer than some of the others. The entrance serves as a foyer with the administrative assistant's desk at the far end.

When she sees us, she jumps to her feet, her eyes wild. Her hair is out of place, her lipstick is a little smeared, and she's clearly agitated. I wonder if someone had just reprimanded her for something, or worse.

"We would like to speak to Terry Treas," I say.

She inhales deeply, holding her breath. Whatever's happening here is above her pay grade, though I wonder how much she actually knows and whether she should be the first one to be interviewed.

"Yes, he's right here," she says. "Terry, there's someone here to speak to you."

"Tell them to get lost. I don't care about Barr or any of his threats! Tell them to leave me alone or I'm going to call the cops," Terry snaps at her.

Will and I exchange looks.

"Actually, sir," I say with a smile at the corner of my lips. "If you're willing to do that right now, we're more than happy to listen."

Terry sticks his head through the doorway. He's a slim man with a crew cut and steely gray eyes. Unlike Barr, he seems humorless and with very little personality.

"You are?" Terry asks.

We introduce ourselves and show him our badges.

"We'd like to speak to you about a few things if you don't mind."

"Yes, sure," he says.

For a moment, I'm surprised by how unbothered he is by our presence here.

I wait for him to lead us to a conference room, but instead, he just walks us back out to the formal foyer and offers us a seat on his stylish but rather uncomfortable couch. The coffee table is styled with unread magazines and a book about fancy old cars called *Speed and The Art of the Performance Automobile*.

"Can Sherry bring you anything to drink?" Terry asks, folding his hands across his knees in a rather awkward manner.

He's dressed in a suit and sits in the suede swivel chair across from us.

"No, I'm good," I say.

"Water, if it's not a problem," Will asks.

Terry motions to Sherry. Will and I talked about the abstract ways where we are going to start the questioning, but not who would actually say something first, so I take the lead.

"We're here to talk to you about certain discrepancies that we have encountered," I begin and then immediately regret starting there.

"Actually, let me start out by telling you that I want to give you my condolences regarding the deaths of Jennifer and Michael Dillard. You were clients of theirs, is that correct?"

"Yes, I can't believe that happened," he says without missing a beat.

"Did you know them well?"

"No, not really. They had a small accounting practice, and so I sort of knew them professionally. They went to a few seminars that we attended, but that's it. We have a bookkeeping company, I don't know if you know that."

"Yes, we do," I say.

"The thing is that we're here to talk to you about the Dillards because we found something very interesting in their office."

"Oh, yes?"

"Yes, something that *you* would find very interesting," Will says.

Terry shrugs his shoulders. "I have no idea what you're talking about."

"There were two sets of books, an online version and a paper version that were associated with your firm, Metcalf Associates."

"My firm?"

"Yes, you *are* the owner of Metcalf Associates, right?"

"Yes, my father-in-law ran the business, but he retired and it's me now."

"Would you have any idea as to why the Dillards would have two sets of books for your company when you're just a small bookkeeping service?"

"No, I have no idea."

"Had you done any business with them before?"

"Yes, we did."

I bring up the folder with the printouts of both the online book and the photocopies of the printed book. When he sees that one, his face turns as white as a sheet, but he immediately denies having any knowledge of it.

"I had no idea that they kept--" Terry starts to say, and then catches himself. "I have no idea what this is."

"You were going to say something else, weren't you?" I ask. "Why did they keep a book like this about your two accounts? I have an idea," I say. "It's a little out there, but it's an idea. You didn't want to report the what, almost two million dollars in income that you actually have. You just wanted to report the small amount of fifty-seven thousand dollars and keep the rest tax-free. But the Dillards, they were smart. They didn't start another online account, they just wrote down the real numbers right here in this paper version as they came in throughout the year with the different dates, with the different pens. We had our experts check it out and it's authentic. It was written at different times and the fingerprints on it match the Dillards. They were the ones who filled it out."

"You said it yourself, they were the ones who filled it out and I had nothing to do with it," Terry says. "Maybe they were framing me or something."

"No, I don't think so," Will says. "I have a feeling that your fingerprints are also going to be found on this book, wouldn't you say? Like the parts on the side where you signed. I'm sure your paw print will show up somewhere, maybe a little residue of your DNA."

"What do you want from me?" Terry asks, his eyes moving frantically from side to side.

He's looking for a way out, I can feel it. Now, what can you tell us to make it all better?

"Terry," I say, taking my time, choosing the words properly. "You are in quite a lot of trouble right now, but you may also have answers to some questions if you're willing to cooperate."

"I had nothing to do with their murder, okay? That money, it's unrelated."

"Really? The books are unrelated?" I ask.

"I'll tell you what you want to know, but only if I get immunity, full immunity."

Will and I exchange looks.

"We'll have to work that out with the attorneys, but first, you have to tell us a little bit about what it is that you think you have to see whether it's worth an immunity."

"What do you want from me? Look, I never meant to keep the double books. It was just something that the Dillards suggested. They thought that I was making too much money and they said why not?"

I don't believe him exactly, but I go along with it. Maybe if he keeps talking, he'll say something that he'll regret.

"I have a question," Will says. "Why is Metcalf Associates listed as the owner of the warehouse that just recently went up in flames out in Desert Rocks?"

He looks at us.

"Oh, you thought that all the records perished in the fire? No, no, they didn't. Just enough have survived to show us that you, or rather Metcalf Associates, was the registered owner and had a license from the city to operate the warehouse, and now it's being investigated as an arson case. Did you start that fire, Terry?"

"No, I had absolutely nothing to do with it."

"Are you in trouble financially? Two million dollars is not enough to live on nowadays?" Will asks sarcastically. "We all know that it's getting expensive out there. The price of housing is going up, inflation. Is that what's going on, you're living above your means? Is that why you had to burn up that warehouse, to try to cash in the insurance money?"

"No, *they* did it to scare me."

The words burst out of him. Will and I look at each other for a moment finding it hard to believe what we *actually* heard.

"Who's after you?" I ask.

"Barr, Barr Houser. He's blackmailing me."

40

CHARLOTTE

I stare at him for a moment. He looks so angry that his body is actually shaking, or is it fear? It's hard to tell sometimes.

"Barr said that everything would be fine, that I would never get in trouble for anything, and yet here we are. Now, he's trying to say that it's all my fault."

Will and I exchange looks. We never want to interfere with the suspect who's angry at someone else and willing to say too much against his own better judgment.

"Barr was the one who probably lit up that warehouse. It was a legitimate business. I was selling stuff on Amazon, notepads, home products, pots and pans, nothing fancy," Terry continues. "I was doing okay and then he came around and said, 'I'm looking for a place to launder my money. I have too much and the cops are after me, and they know that I can't possibly afford that house on my nonexistent salary, and so they're searching for it.' When I told him no, he made threats. He said I do it or he'd kill my family. I had no choice."

"Okay, go on. Do you want some water?" Will asks.

"No, I have to get this out," Terry says, his face red with anger. "He threatened my wife. He said it'd be terrible if something were to happen to her on the way home from work. She's a freaking bookkeeper. That's all we were and then he came around and he got us involved in this mess."

"What mess?" I ask. "What happened exactly?"

"He needed to launder his drug money. He had so much and he thought that a bookkeeper with a warehouse was the way to do it. I mean, I had a great business, right? Only, it didn't make that much money. It broke even, but that's about it. I wasn't good at picking just the right products to sell and the whole warehouse thing was a disaster. I should have just kept it. I should have just had Amazon do the fulfillment, but I thought I could save a few pennies and look what happened."

"So you're saying that he torched it?" I ask. "There's no way this was an accident?"

"He said that he would," Terry says. "I have him on video."

My mouth drops open. I had expected possibly a confession, maybe a few lies here and there, but a recording?

"After he threatened my wife, I started recording everything he said to me," Terry explains. "He didn't know this, of course, but I set up a small hidden camera in the office and I just wanted to make sure that I got everything, just in case. I have it all backed up, too."

"We'd like to see that, of course. But first, tell us everything," Will says.

"The Dillards weren't cooperating, they were involved as well. He had them launder money, lie on the returns but there were some audits with the IRS, and their names were on them. They told Barr that they were going to cooperate. That was a stupid thing to do. They should have just told the IRS everything, and then split, left town or something but they were angry. He basically bullied them into this position. First, giving them business, lying to them, having them sign books, and approve accounting that didn't make sense.

Then, when they wanted to go back on it, when they wanted to tell the IRS the truth, Barr threatened them."

"Did he kill them?" I ask.

"I don't know. I'm assuming yes, but I don't know for sure. I didn't see it if that's what you're asking."

"Okay. Keep going," I say, taking a sip of Will's water. My mouth is growing parched.

I started out taking notes but gave up and just set my phone to record. This was too much information to absorb.

"He was involved with it all. Barr was in a lot of trouble," Terry says. "He escaped that one murder case, but there was another one. He got wind that it's going to get made."

I look at Will with surprise.

"I think you might be mistaken," Will says, shaking his head.

"It's not in this county. It's in Riverside," Terry explains. "Barr is all pissed off over it. He wanted to tie up all the loose ends. The problem is that one of the loose ends was the Dillards."

"What do you mean?" I ask.

"They were there when he made threats against that person, and then they were talking to the IRS and the cops. He just snapped."

"Is that so?"

"You know that he's capable of anything, right? I mean, that murder case that he got off on a few years back, that was just like one of thirty. Everyone knows that, anyone who has worked with him. He paid off a bunch of cops in your department. You know which ones those are?"

Will and I exchange looks.

"I've never-- No, I don't but I'd love to know," I say.

"No, I can't have the cops turning on me, too. It sounds like a veiled threat and maybe he's exaggerating, but I can't know for sure. If you want to see the videos, I have them in my office, but you're going to give me immunity, right? I'm fighting for my life here. If I cooperate with you and I work for the police, he's going to try to kill me and my wife."

"We're going to talk to the DA and we can get you protection," I say, "But yes, we want to see those videos."

A few hours later, we manage to look through each one. They were long and tedious but he fast forwards to the good bits, and by good, I mean excellent.

There's Barr making threats against him. There's Barr telling him that something bad is going to happen to the warehouse if he doesn't help him get out of this. Then, there's him ranting and railing about the Dillards cooperating with the IRS and the cops.

From the videos, I can tell that, at one point, Barr and Terry were close friends. They made an odd couple. Barr is gregarious, big in size, the kind of man who looks like he knows how to have a good time, and Terry is small, diminutive, serious, the kind of man whose idea of a good time is staying home with a good book.

At the end of the day, with our stomachs growling from lack of food, Will and I both know that Terry's telling the truth. At first, I thought the fear was an act, but then I realized that when we showed up here, it was a relief. He no longer needed to go to the police.

We're here to help him. We happened to show up at the right time, putting him in the right frame of mind to share everything that he knows. After we transfer over all of the video evidence onto the hard drive that we find in the car, we tell Terry to follow us back to the station.

I offer to give him a ride but he's afraid.

"It will be best if I follow you and then maybe if Barr has anyone watching me, I can leave and it will look like I talk to you but I'm not being held or anything like that. What about my wife?"

"We have a deputy picking her up right now."

"Good," Terry says. "Thanks."

He seems relieved.

"We're going to put you both in a motel at an undisclosed location. Far away. We can switch cars if we need to. We're going to make sure you have no tail. No one's going to know where you are and you're going to be safe," I say.

"Good." He nods. "Because everyone else who even made a threat against him ended up dead."

"It's not going to happen to you, Terry," I say. "We're going to put a lot of manpower on you to protect you and we have the video evidence now as well as your testimony. We need to get your official statement at the station. Everything is going to be okay. Do you want to stop by somewhere and get some food first? Something at a drive-thru?"

"Okay, let's go together just to be safe. You can follow behind us. Are you sure you don't want to go in our car?" I ask again.

"Yes, I'm fine. I want to have a car anyway."

"You won't be able to take it to your motel. They'll be able to trail you. You'll have to leave it at the station," Will says.

"Yes, I understand." He nods. "But like I said before, I just don't want him to think that you're taking me there against my will or I'm being forced to cooperate or anything like that."

"I understand. That's probably the best way to play it," I agree.

Just as we're about to walk out, Will stops for a moment and asks, "But what about the missing teeth?"

Terry looks up at him.

"The Dillards had three teeth pulled after they were dead. Made it seem like a serial killer or someone in training to be one was involved. Someone doing it for sadistic rather than business purposes."

"I don't know." Terry shakes his head, looking surprised.

"Does that sound like something that Barr would do?"

"I have no idea. I mean, maybe. I thought they were just shot."

"Yes, we kept that evidence out, just in case."

Will and I exchange looks. I don't know if his reaction means anything at all. Probably not, but I'm glad that Will brought it up.

Why pull their teeth after all? Why pull their teeth if it's not some sadistic pleasure-seeking behavior? If it's just business, why go to that extra length? It's not exactly commonplace. With that thought, still firmly in my mind, we get into our car.

41

CHARLOTTE

With my stomach doing rolls, I realize that I haven't eaten since this morning. My mouth salivates at the prospect of getting some food. Frenchy's drive-thru is unfortunately packed. I text Terry to ask if he minds stopping by the Coffee Break.

"No, I love that place," he texts back and we go around the corner.

The line is a few cars less, but still significant. We get in line and get ready for the long wait. As it crawls over to the order window and I ask for two orders of egg bites, as well as a chocolate croissant, Will jokes about my lack of proper eating habits.

"Why don't you get a sandwich or something substantial?"

"This will do. I think after the conversation we had, I deserve a little bit of a celebratory croissant," I say.

"They never put enough chocolate in that. You think it's going to be filled but it's always lacking."

"Listen, I didn't complain about your soda drinking in the car."

"Actually, yes, you did." He smiles.

"I think that you need to give me some leeway here. That was quite a meeting that we had and evidence that we found."

"Yes, can you believe all that? You think he's telling the truth?"

"He seems scared and will say just about anything, including the truth."

"But is he really telling the truth? Any chance that he could be the one that's actually behind all this, his name is on the warehouse. He could have torched it himself. Barr would be an excellent scapegoat."

"I guess, except for Barr does have a history of murdering a lot of people and getting away with it. He probably wouldn't be on my top list of people to turn on."

"Maybe not, but think about it," Will says. "He's the perfect person to make an accusation about. Terry knows that the department all hates him. We know that he committed a bajillion different crimes that we can't really get him on. He's the perfect person to frame."

"What about all those conversations on video?" I ask.

"Yes, that's true. We have to go through them. Terry did fast forward to the really juicy parts related to his case, but there is a whole bunch of video there that we didn't see."

"So, you don't believe him?" I ask.

"I don't know. Maybe I'm just searching for something that we overlooked. Is it really as simple as this guy confessing and the case is solved?"

"Sometimes it is," I say. "Sometimes it's really the bad guy that did it. Actually, no. *Most* of the time, it is actually the bad guy that did it. He's the one who's responsible. The evidence lines up. There isn't some spooky alternative solution, big surprise ending. Books, movies, yes, but real-life police work? We build a case one kernel of evidence after another, and that's what you get."

"But what about your gut?" Will asks.

"My gut? My gut says that Barr's the one who did it. I would also add that Terry may have had something to do with it. Perhaps he's not as innocent in the whole money laundering/hiding assets from the IRS scheme as he wants us to believe. We have a whole bunch of paperwork to go through before we can come to that conclusion."

Just as we pull up to the window to get our order, I hear some yelling behind me. Terry's car is behind ours and in front of a large Cadillac SUV.

The tussle is coming from the outside. When I look back, I see two men dressed in casual business attire, pointing their guns at Terry, who is outside his vehicle.

His hands are raised and protesting. One of the men is yelling something at him.

Terry takes a few steps closer to them with his hands covering his face.

I jump out of the car.

"You come with us now or you're going to get shot." I hear one of them say. "Let's go."

It's the side of the building and no one is around, except for the line of cars in the drive-thru. The line was snaked around the corner and now it's just our three cars on this side.

A black Toyota is parked nearby. One of the men is trying to pull Terry into it.

"Help! I had nothing to do with this. Stop it. I'm not going with you!" he yells, taking a few steps forward, as they brandish the gun in his face.

"Put your weapon down!" I yell, positioning myself behind the car, just in case. "Now!"

"Police!" Will yells.

Without any further protest, the guy closest to me shoots Terry in the forehead.

One shot.

I unload my gun into his chest and Will shoots his partner. They fall onto the ground, their bodies littered with bullets.

Right next to them, Terry Treas looks up at the deep blue sky and takes his last breath.

"Oh my God! What the hell was that?" I ask, stunned for a moment.

Will reaches over, calls for backup, and makes all of the necessary reports on the radio.

Backup arrives a few minutes later to secure the scene and push a few looky-loos and shocked witnesses to the other side of the building where they can't see the bodies.

Will and I are quickly separated, and our stories are taken. Internal Affairs shows up with their crime scene investigators, and our questioning goes on for a good couple of hours.

While the scene is processed, no identification is found on the two men who were trying to get Terry into their car. A couple of deputies quickly recognize them as men who work for Barr Houser. They have a few arrests, nothing major, driving under the influence and loitering. They were known associates, drug dealers/low-level guys doing Barr's dirty work.

Will and I don't talk again that evening, and I return home stunned and lost, uncertain as to where to go from here. Luckily, I have the recording of what Terry said to us, as well as the hard drive with the recordings from Terry's conversations with Barr, but still not an eyewitness, and who knows what things will be admissible or kicked out of court completely.

That night, I fall into a deep sleep. The much-needed rest is somewhere right out of reach. I toss and turn, and my thoughts keep coming back to what I could have done to prevent all of this from happening.

What if Terry had traveled with us in the same vehicle? Maybe then they wouldn't have tried to take him. Or maybe they would've shot us dead right then and there?

All of these thoughts keep me up, and a few hours before dawn, I give up, get up, and start the day.

42

CHARLOTTE

The following morning, I meet with the lieutenant in his office to talk about the shooting. Will is already there. We gave our formal statements yesterday, and this is the first time that I've seen him. He looks tired, a little on edge, and exactly how I feel.

"They're doing the raid on Barr Houser's house as we speak. He's already in custody as of about an hour ago," the lieutenant notifies us.

"But we're not there," I say.

"You can't be there. You were involved in a shooting. You had to use your weapons. Internal Affairs has to investigate everything that happened prior to you returning to work. You know how it is."

"We could have at least been there," Will moans.

"Yes, but I thought tensions would be a lot lower if you weren't."

"God, Lieutenant," Will says, "I can't believe that this is happening already and we missed it."

"You two have done enough."

The lieutenant stands up, clearly not taking the intimidation tactic from Will.

"I'm sorry," Will says. "It's just that we worked on this case and Barr was a big part of it."

"As you know, this department has been after Barr for a long time. A number of cases didn't stick. This one hopefully will. He's in custody, handcuffs on, but he's still at his house. We're doing the search while he's there. Maybe he'll crack and talk before that attorney of his shows up, but who knows? He's probably too smart for that."

The lieutenant looks tired, worn out. I know that he's been on the phone with nearby sheriff's departments all morning, if not all night, talking about the raid and planning what to do.

A part of me feels like I'm missing out on something but another part is frankly relieved. The shooting shook me. I didn't want to kill anyone. Frankly, I'm still pissed off at those two men for making me pull the trigger. I get no satisfaction from anything like that. I saw their faces all night long and probably will for days to come.

" In a few hours, they're going to bring Barr in," the lieutenant says, "and you can be here to watch the interrogation."

"Watch?" Will asks. "We were the ones who did all of the work on this case."

"My hands are tied and you know that. You two are on leave until those shootings are cleared."

"Are you sure that we will be?" I ask.

"There were cameras everywhere with plenty footage of what happened."

"Can't you wait to do the interrogation until *after* we're cleared?" Will asks.

"No, the sooner, the better. It will give Barr less time to come up with a better story, work on something with his lawyer. You know he's not one to say a word and so I doubt that the interrogation is going to produce much fruit anyway. I've got to make more calls. I'll talk to you two later."

Right before we walk out of his office, I turn around and ask about Terry's wife.

"She's fine," Lieutenant Soderman says. "A deputy took her to a motel room. Nothing unusual happened. I guess they weren't coordinated enough to try to get her as well."

"Does she know about Terry?" I ask.

"She was notified and became distraught. We'll see if there's anything more that she is willing to share with us now that her husband was murdered."

I follow Will out to the station and the loud hum that generally prevails in the room dies down for a moment.

Everyone quiets down and watches us for a second.

I've talked to a few people about what happened one on one, but at this moment it feels like I'm expected to make some sort of speech. Instead, I go to my desk and Will follows.

There's a little bit of privacy there and I recline into the chair that is less than comfortable. Recently I've had a lot of backaches from sitting too long and the stakeout surely didn't help matters. I try to do a little bit of stretching.

I know that the sciatica pain won't go away unless I actually get some physical exercise and a few sessions of yoga.

"I can't believe that we can't be there. They're doing all of this without us," Will says.

"Come on, you can't be serious." I shake my head, turning on my computer to go through the piles and piles of emails that I still have to get through.

"Yes, I know. I just thought that putting up a stink would make me look more involved."

"You're already involved, you shot one of his men. That's how involved you are. Now we have IA on our butts explaining what happened."

"Nothing. We had no choice, you know that," Will says. "This isn't even one of those other types of shootings where anything can be debated. They actually shot him and pointed their guns at us."

"I just hope those cameras out there were working and there's enough corroboration with our story, not just our word."

"The lieutenant seems to think so."

"I'm not *really* worried," I say after a moment. "On the other hand, we don't have to handle the rest of this case, which is a little freeing."

"Yes, I guess." Will shrugs. "Then again, I've always been a much harder worker than you have."

He gives me a wink and I force a smile. I've missed his banter. Things have been utterly too serious between us for a little too long. I'm tempted to ask him about Erin but this isn't the right time or place.

"What are you going to do with your couple of days off?" he asks.

"I think we have the meetings with Internal Affairs later today but you know it always takes them a few working days to make a decision. There's the weekend coming up, as well. I doubt we'll hear anything until Tuesday. What are you planning to do?" I ask.

"Since I do have paid time off, I'm thinking of going to the beach, actually. It's only a two-hour drive. A couple of days with sand in between my toes and the smell of salt air. I think it could do me some good."

"You interested in bringing anyone along, anyone special?" I ask, already knowing the answer to this question.

"Maybe." He smiles back. "Listen, you should go ahead and take advantage, too. Maybe you and Dylan can go away somewhere, even if it's just a hotel."

"I don't know if we're there yet," I say.

"Didn't you already go on a trip with him?"

"Yes, but it was a day trip."

"Make it an overnight." He winks.

"Why are you still keen on me getting a better love life?"

"Because I feel bad for you just moping around, wasting all these days off. You don't get that many, you know."

"Maybe I will," I say with a nod. "That does sound nice."

43

CHARLOTTE

The rest of the day in the office goes by at a snail's pace, punctuated by periods of excitement. Barr is brought into the interrogation room. His lawyer is with him , naturally. A couple of different detectives take their opportunity to interview, all to no avail.

He sees me on the way and actually gives me a wink. I guess his lawyer has identified me as one of the detectives who killed his men. Barr's arrogance is without limits, but that's okay. The law may move slowly, but it's a force to be reckoned with. We keep chipping away and eventually get what we want, one way or another.

I talk to the investigators who come in for a break from searching Barr's house.

"So far, we haven't found much," one of them says. "But maybe he wasn't keeping anything incriminating at his house. There're a number of businesses registered to him and who knows where else? We'll keep at it," he promises.

"I'm sure you'll find something," I reassure him even though I'm anything but certain of that.

When Terry's wife is brought in for a chat, her face is ashen from the news of her husband's death and her willowy frame looks like she could be knocked over by a breeze. Afterward, Marilyn emerges with a satisfied smile on her face.

"We're working on an immunity deal," she says. "Terry had a lot of files in his home office and kept track of everything. He was the diligent kind."

"What does that mean exactly?" I ask.

"She's pissed off and willing to provide all evidence and testimony if we work with the IRS and make sure she doesn't have do any time on the tax evasion."

"Do you think they are going to go for it?" I ask.

"There will be heavy penalties and she'll have to pay back everything that she's owes plus interest and fees, but when I talked to the agents on the phone they seemed amenable. They wouldn't have a case without ours and a tax thief is not as bad as a murderer of multiple people. A drug dealer definitely trumps a tax thief."

"What about her story?" I ask.

Marilyn looks directly into my eyes. "She didn't have a chance to talk to Terry before his death but she confirmed almost everything that he said."

"Really?"

"Yes. They were bullied into giving over their warehouse. There were a lot of threats. One building on the other. They had no recourse because they lied about the money. They were afraid to go to the authorities. I believe her and you should, too. They were greedy but they didn't want to have anyone murdered or hurt."

"Okay," I say.

Marilyn is usually a stickler for the truth and hates getting into deals with people who she suspects of being involved in even the slightest way. Given the fact that his wife had said the exact same thing that Terry told us, I believe her as well.

My conversation with Internal Affairs goes well. I repeat what happened a couple of times, refusing to take my lawyer's advice and not saying anything until the video comes back.

Luckily, it shows up right at the end of my interrogation. Everyone in the room watches it with bated breath, except for me because I already know what's on it.

At the end of the day, right before I'm about to close my computer and leave the rest of the work for another day, I hear a commotion at the lieutenant's office.

People start to gather around. The two detectives assigned to the case after us and Marilyn are there already.

"What's going on?" I ask, following suit.

"Not sure exactly," someone says.

We stand right outside while the lieutenant tells us all to be quiet so he can hear. Then he puts the phone on speaker.

"Okay, Deputy, take a deep breath and repeat what you just said."

The lieutenant puts his finger to his lips and a hush comes over the room.

I have no idea who is calling or why we're all gathered here, but it can't be that important, I say to myself. Barr Houser had gotten away with a lot of murders, one that went all the way to trial. Without solid proof, his lawyer will probably wiggle him out of this case as well. With Terry dead, there's no eyewitness testimony. Who knows what doubts his attorney can cast on the videos that were collected and found?

Terry's wife is here to testify. While everyone else seems to be elated by that fact, I'm still feeling at a loss and unwilling to celebrate the end of the case.

They found no solid proof so far at his house. To actually pin the murder of the Dillards on him without a gun, without any concrete evidence, no eyewitnesses, no video tapes, no DNA, no bodily fluids, how's that even going to work?

If anything, Barr might possibly get some time for ordering the kidnapping and the killing of Terry Treas, but even that would be a hard case to make.

"I'm here," the deputy on the phone says after a bit of commotion on his end.

"Sorry, we were just making sure that all the evidence was stored properly in evidence bags."

"Are you recording the chain of evidence? No one touched it without recording it, right?" the lieutenant asks.

I look at Will. What could he possibly be talking about?

"Yes, we got it all right here."

364

"What? What do you have?" I ask. There's a brief pause on the other end.

"The teeth," the deputy says. "We found two matchboxes containing three teeth each."

My mouth drops open.

"The boxes are labeled with Jennifer Dillard and Michael Dillard's names in what looks to be Barr's handwriting, but of course we still have to confirm that."

The silence that just fell over the office gets filled with noise. So many people start talking at once that the lieutenant tells us all to get the heck out so he can hear the deputy.

"They found the teeth," Will says, looking at me. "That's a nail in the coffin. We've got him."

I smile ear to ear and a wave of relief washes over me.

We got him.

We actually got him.

44

CHARLOTTE

I meet up with Dylan after work and tell him the good news. He gives me a celebratory hug and kiss and asks about my meeting with Internal Affairs.

"I just went through the story a couple of times. I had my attorney. I don't expect any issues since there's video evidence of what happened. The whole shooting was caught on the security cameras which, surprisingly, had the sound recording, as well."

"Wow, really?"

"They apparently had a few problems with unhappy customers making scenes about their frosted lattes or whatever so they upgraded their security cameras just in time."

"That's good," Dylan says. "What a relief for you both."

"Yes, it is."

We have dinner at a favorite Thai restaurant of mine that he has never been to. It's casual but the food is excellent and I've been famished all day.

"Hey, listen, I've been thinking about Kelsey Hall," he says when our food arrives.

His hair falls slightly into his face. He'd recently taken a shower after another long day that started at 4:00 a.m. but he looks refreshed.

"I'm off over the next couple of days and I know you are, too."

I nod.

"Well, I was thinking that you're curious about Kelsey. Jonathan says it's her, but how can we believe that? How can it actually be her if the DNA doesn't match?"

"Maybe she would know," I say.

"She doesn't have many memories from that time. But she remembers that concert. She may remember you. Who knows?"

"What are you trying to get at here, Dylan?" I ask.

"Well, I was just thinking about maybe setting up a video call with her but that wouldn't be as conclusive as an in-person meeting."

"I don't even know if she'd want to talk to me."

"If you just showed up at her house, maybe she would. She was trying to get her parents to believe her, right? Maybe it'd be good to have someone who'd be able to tell if it's actually her."

I think about it for a moment. "What do you want to do?"

"Well, she lives in Las Vegas. What is that, three hours from here? We can make a trip out of it. You, me, a couple of days by the pool and in the casino. We can have some fun. We can gamble. We can also go see about Kelsey."

"That sounds-- Yes, maybe." I nod, considering his proposition.

"I'll take a maybe." Dylan reaches over the table and squeezes my hand. "Do you want to go?"

I give him a smile. "Okay, let's do it."

THANK YOU FOR READING! I hope you enjoyed the second Detective Charlotte Pierce novel. Cant' wait to read more? **Dive into Missing Lives now!**

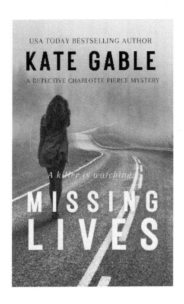

When two young boys disappear while riding their bikes, Detective Charlotte Pierce must follow the clues to find their killer before he strikes again.

In the dusty outskirts of Mesquite County, California, two kids go missing, taken from outside their homes. The quiet desert community is devastated and it's up to Charlotte to find out what happened.

The FBI is called in and a man who stalked and terrorized Charlotte comes back into her

life. She kept his secret to protect her career, but is now being forced to work with him to solve the case.

What happens when she confronts him about what he has done? What happens when the killer start searching for another victim?

1-click Missing Lives now!

IF YOU ENJOYED THIS BOOK, please take a moment to write a short review on your favorite book site and maybe recommend it to a friend or two.

DON'T WANT to wait until the new release and want to dive into another series right now? Make sure to grab **GIRL HIDDEN (a novella) for FREE!**

A family is found dead in their home. The only survivor is the teenage daughter who managed to escape the burning house.

Who killed them? And why? **Detective Kaitlyn Carr has to bring their killer to justice.**

A year before her disappearance, Violet, Kaitlyn's sister, comes to stay with her after a bad fight with their mom. She can't stand living at home as much as Kaitlyn once did and wants to move in with her.

What happens when the dysfunction of her own family threatens to blow up her face and let the killer off for good?

GRAB GIRL HIDDEN for FREE now!

IF YOU ENJOYED THIS BOOK, please take a moment to write a short review on your favorite book site and maybe recommend it to a friend or two.

You can also join my Facebook group, Kate Gable's Reader Club, for exclusive giveaways and sneak peeks of future books.

BE THE FIRST TO KNOW ABOUT MY UPCOMING SALES, NEW RELEASES AND EXCLUSIVE GIVEAWAYS!

W ant a Free book? Sign up for my Newsletter!

Sign up for my newsletter:

https://www.subscribepage.com/kategableviplist

Join my Facebook Group:
https://www.facebook.com/
groups/833851020557518

Bonus Points: Follow me on BookBub and
Goodreads!

https://www.goodreads.com/author/show/
21534224.Kate_Gable

ABOUT KATE GABLE

Kate Gable loves a good mystery that is full of suspense. She grew up devouring psychological thrillers and crime novels as well as movies, tv shows and true crime.

Her favorite stories are the ones that are centered on families with lots of secrets and lies as well as many twists and turns. Her novels have elements of psychological suspense, thriller, mystery and romance.

Kate Gable lives near Palm Springs, CA with her husband, son, a dog and a cat. She has spent more than twenty years in Southern California and finds inspiration from its cities, canyons, deserts, and small mountain towns.

She graduated from University of Southern California with a Bachelor's degree in Mathematics. After pursuing graduate studies in mathematics, she switched gears and got her MA in Creative Writing and English from Western New Mexico University and her PhD in Education from Old Dominion University.

Writing has always been her passion and obsession. Kate is also a USA Today Bestselling author of romantic suspense under another pen name.

Write her here:

Kate@kategable.com

Check out her books here:

www.kategable.com

Sign up for my newsletter:
https://www.subscribepage.com/kategableviplist

Join my Facebook Group:
https://www.facebook.com/
groups/833851020557518

Bonus Points: Follow me on BookBub and Goodreads!

https://www.bookbub.com/authors/kate-gable

https://www.goodreads.com/author/show/
21534224.Kate_Gable

amazon.com/Kate-Gable/e/B095XFCLL7

facebook.com/kategablebooks

bookbub.com/authors/kate-gable

instagram.com/kategablebooks

ALSO BY KATE GABLE

All books are available at ALL major retailers! If you can't find it, please email me at
kate@kategable.com

Detective Kaitlyn Carr

Girl Missing (Book 1) - FREE for a Limited Time!

Girl Lost (Book 2)
Girl Found (Book 3)
Girl Taken (Book 4)
Girl Forgotten (Book 5)
Girl Hidden (FREE Novella)

Detective Charlotte Pierce

Last Breath
Nameless Girl
Missing Lives